OCTR 1998

NO LONGER PROPERTY OF
SPRINGFIELD-GREENE CO. LIBRARY

THE
PINK RABBIT
CAPER

THE PINK RABBIT CAPER

•

(Book Eleven)
in
The Jennifer Gray
Veterinarian Mystery
Series

•

GEORGETTE LIVINGSTON

AVALON BOOKS
THOMAS BOUREGY AND COMPANY, INC.
401 LAFAYETTE STREET
NEW YORK, NEW YORK 10003

SPRINGFIELD-GREENE COUNTY LIBRARY
SPRINGFIELD, MISSOURI

© Copyright 1998 by Georgette Livingston
Library of Congress Catalog Card Number 97-97118
ISBN 0-8034-9279-0
All rights reserved.
All the characters in this book are fictitious,
and any resemblance to actual persons,
living or dead, is purely coincidental.

FIRST PRINTING

PRINTED IN THE UNITED STATES OF AMERICA
ON ACID-FREE PAPER
BY HADDON CRAFTSMEN, BLOOMSBURG, PENNSYLVANIA

For Shelby Marie, who prefers purple to pink

Chapter One

As Jennifer Gray walked along the pathway toward Calico House, she lifted her face to the soft breeze coming in off White River, and breathed in deeply of the sweet scent of flowers and freshly cut grass. It was springtime, that wonderful time of year when wildflowers still covered the countryside in profusion, and the gardens around town burst forth with color and foliage. And nowhere was it more apparent than here, in Calico Park. It had been an ideal location to build the senior citizens' center, and although most of the functions at the center were for the older generation, the writing class Jennifer had been attending for the past two weeks with Emma Morrison was open to anyone who had the burning desire to learn to write. Well, the ''burning desire'' was Emma's, not hers, but the class was only two hours long on Tuesday and Thursday nights, and had sounded like fun, so she'd signed up, too, much to her grandfather's delight and encouragement. Jennifer suspected the real reason for his gentle urging was the fact that he thought she needed a little R and R, after going through a grueling month of nearly nonstop work at the animal clinic, while her partner, Ben Copeland, recovered from a broken leg.

Jennifer smiled, whispering the word ''partner,'' as though it were a soft, sweet song. Ben had given her the job as his assistant at the clinic just as soon as she'd gotten home from veterinary school, and always with the thought in mind that when he retired, she would continue on, managing his practice. And so it was more than a surprise when Ben suggested they become equal partners legally. It hardly seemed fair, after he'd spent so many years struggling to fulfill his dream, and so she had agreed only if he would let her buy in, no matter how long it took. But oh, how flattered she had been that he'd had that kind of faith in her, and how proud she was now to be the co-owner of the Front Street Veterinary Clinic.

Jennifer had reached the low, sprawling building, and after walking through the reception area, she quickly made her way down the hall to the meeting room. Their instructor, Judith Stoker, an ex-librarian, was trying to explain the elements of style, and why omitting needless words was so important in any writing endeavor.

"Sorry I'm late," Jennifer said to Judith, as she slipped into the chair beside Emma. "But I had an emergency at the clinic."

Judith Stoker was a stern-looking woman with battleship gray hair, piercing dark eyes, and a square jaw that jutted out when she was upset or angry. In some ways, she looked a lot like her husband, who was one of the two judges in town, and both husband and wife were formidable.

And Judith's jaw was jutting out now, as she frowned at Jennifer. "I am aware you are a busy young woman, Jennifer, what with Ben Copeland laid up with a broken leg, but tardiness sets the whole class back." She looked at her watch. "You've missed fifteen minutes."

Jennifer managed a smile. "I don't expect you to go back and recap on my account, Mrs. Stoker. Whatever I missed, I'll get from Emma."

Judith made a face. "Well, good luck! Emma has been so busy working on her little contribution to our first reading session, she hasn't heard one thing I've said."

Emma, who had a head of brown curly hair, bright blue, expressive eyes, and a beautiful, almost unlined face, could be a bit formidable, too. She said with a snort, "I've heard every word you've said, Judith, so why don't you just get on with it. In case you haven't noticed, you've just wasted a good three minutes prattling."

Whispers and titters followed, as the students tried for composure. In turn, Judith's frown deepened. "Then suppose you tell us why omitting needless words is so important, Emma."

Emma drew a "smiley" face at the top of one of her papers, changed the mouth to droop downward, and muttered, "A sentence should contain no unnecessary words, and a paragraph no unnecessary sentences. In other words, instead of rambling, get to it, and say what you mean."

"Can you give us an example of that?"

"Uh-huh. Let's start with your last sentence. Last two words, 'of that.' You didn't need to tag that on, Judith. 'Can you give us an example?' would have done it."

Titters again, and Judith squared her shoulders. "What about you, Nettie? Can you give us an example we'd be more familiar with? Possibly one out of Strunk and White's book, *The Elements of Style*?"

While Nettie gave the woman the example she wanted, Jennifer took a deep breath, and tried to relax. It hadn't been her fault she'd had an emergency at the clinic at the last minute that had required surgery.

She'd called Emma to tell her she wouldn't be home for dinner, and would have to go straight to class from the clinic, and now, her stomach was rumbling in protest.

Emma heard the grumbling sounds, and reached into her purse. "Thought you might be hungry," she whispered, handing Jennifer a sandwich, "so I brought along a ham sandwich, cut up into bite-sized pieces. You should be able to get it down without the old barracuda catching on."

Jennifer grinned, and gave Emma a quick hug. "I love you."

"And I love you, too," Emma returned, giving her a conspiratorial wink.

And it was true. Jennifer did love Emma with all her heart. Emma had been her grandfather's housekeeper for years, and had helped raise her after her parents' untimely death. She'd only been eight at the time, and had felt so lost and alone, she'd clung to Emma and Wes, desperately needing their love and understanding. Now, they shared the comfortable old house that was nestled beside Calico Christian Church, where Jennifer's grandfather was pastor, and they were a true family, loving and giving in every way.

Jennifer looked around the room, and took inventory of the students who were seated at the oversized wooden tables. In a way, she supposed she loved all of them, because they were a part of the wonderful memories that made up Calico's past, as well as its dreams for the future.

First, there was Nettie Balkin, who had been Sheriff Cody's dispatcher, secretary, and clerk for almost as long as he had been sheriff. And like Judith and her husband, Nettie and the sheriff looked a lot alike, too, with heads of gray hair and rotund bodies. Nettie was a widow, but the sheriff was married to prim and proper Ida, who hated everything about police work, and was continually after Jim to retire.

Nora Muller, an attractive woman in her mid-fifties, was sitting on Nettie's right, plump Mrs. Wiggs on her left, and Orris Ford, the town butcher, was sitting across from Mrs. Wiggs, looking pretty depressed, because he was the only man in the class. He had made it clear the first night that unless another man or two signed up, he was dropping out. But he was still in class, so Jennifer could only assume he was getting something out of it.

Mildred Wilson, mother of the troublemaking Wilson brothers, sat at the far table with Meg Ashton, Lenora Hyde, and Tracy Madison, and last but not least, Lolly Peabody had taken the seat across from Emma. Jennifer was wondering how anybody could possibly describe eccentric, silver-haired Lolly, who wore clothes out of the twenties, and carried around the large, stuffed pink rabbit her husband had given her the Easter before he died, when she caught the woman's eyes on her, and the look of cunning amusement on her dimpled face. She'd been watching every secret mouthful Jennifer took, and Jennifer felt a flush sweep her cheeks.

Lolly winked, gave Jennifer a thumbs-up sign, and went back to listening to Judith, who was now discussing how important it was *not* to take shortcuts at the cost of clarity. Jennifer found herself wondering just how that worked if you were supposed to

The Pink Rabbit Caper

omit needless words, but you weren't supposed to take shortcuts?

And then Judith said, "If you are writing about the F.B.I., don't use the initials. Simply call it the Federal Bureau of Investigation. That's what I mean by clarity. Don't expect your readers to be mind readers."

Jennifer shoved the last of the sandwich in her mouth, and sighed. There was so much to learn, she didn't think she was ever going to get the hang of it. Not that it mattered. She had no intentions of taking writing on as a career, or even as a hobby. Emma, on the other hand, who was an avid mystery reader, had been talking about writing a mystery for ages, and took the whole thing very seriously, which was one of the reasons why she was concentrating more on the papers in front of her than on what Judith was saying. This was the night everybody was supposed to bring something to read, something they'd written, and Emma had been working on the opening of her story for a week.

Judith said, "We'll be able to get into

the subject of style a little more thoroughly as each of you read what you've written. And remember, this is a fiction class. It's quite normal, and logical, for a beginning writer to write about what they know. And usually it's preferred. But just remember, if any of you have done that, make sure you've turned it into fiction.

"We'll begin with you, Meg. I'm just taking a guess, here, but inasmuch as your son was recently elected mayor, I have the feeling he'll be the focus of your story."

"As a matter of fact, he isn't," Meg said, standing up. "Not that Willy isn't the most important person in my life, but my parrot, Scamp, won out. He's wonderfully unique, and every day with him is an adventure. Unfortunately, I still don't have anything down on paper." Meg ran a hand through her dark, curly hair in frustration. "I just don't think I'm going to be very good at this, Judith. I've made several attempts, and they've all ended up in the wastebasket."

Judith looked around and sighed. "Do

we have any 'attempts' that *didn't* end up in the wastebasket?''

"I wrote a poem," Nettie grumbled. "Wouldn't that be considered fiction?"

"*Is* it fiction?"

"Well, no, not exactly."

Judith waved a hand in frustration. "We all know, by her own admission, that Emma is writing a masterpiece, but what about the rest of you?"

Lolly said, "I wrote a poem, too, but it's about a little dog I had years ago."

Mrs. Wiggs said, "I wrote a little something about Sir Scuffy, but I suppose that isn't fiction, either."

Judith sighed. "I know most of you have pets, and I understand why you would want to write about them, but unless you've put them into a fictional situation . . ."

Lolly spoke up again. "Why don't you let Emma read the beginning of her mystery, Judith? She seems to be the only one here who knows what she's doing."

Heads bobbed in agreement, and Judith looked at Emma levelly. "So, are you ready, Emma?"

Emma nodded, and stood up. When the room grew silent, she said, "I guess you all know by now, I'm writing a mystery story. I'm calling it 'Deadly Harvest,' though I might change the title later on. It's about a lady who was married five times, killed all her husbands, and planted them in her rose garden."

Lenora Hyde, who weighed at least two hundred and fifty pounds, fanned her face with a pink hanky, and gasped. "Goodness, Emma. That's *ghastly!*"

Emma smiled pertly. "Uh-huh, but it got your attention, didn't it? I'm setting the story in a town called White River...."

Mrs. Wiggs waved a hand. "Which means it's really Calico, and you've just changed the name."

Judith snapped, "Let Emma get on with this, or we'll be here all night!"

Emma cleared her throat. "Okay, so the town is called White River. My protagonist—"

Mildred Wilson broke in. "Your *what?*"

Judith rolled her eyes. "That subject was

The Pink Rabbit Caper

covered during our first class, Mildred and, as I recall, you were sitting right there."

"My principal character," Emma said. "My protagonist is a private detective named Jake Lamont. The story begins on a sunny Monday morning in July, when Jake receives an anonymous call informing him that there have been five murders, and the bodies have been buried somewhere in town. Jake thinks it's a crank call until the next morning, when he receives a clue in the mail, which will be the first of many. Each clue will bring Jake a little closer to finding the bodies, and..."

"Who are you thinking about for the part of Jake Lamont?" Orris asked.

Lolly giggled. "You thinking of trying out for the part, Orris? Well, you'd better lose that belly and grow some hair."

It was Emma's turn to roll her eyes. "I'm not casting a play or a movie, Orris Ford. I'm simply writing a mystery story." She looked at Judith. "I'm ready to read the first few pages."

Judith sat down and sighed. "Go ahead,

Emma. You obviously have everybody's attention."

Emma began:

My name is Jake Lamont. I'm a private detective in the small town of White River, Nebraska. I would probably make more money if I moved to a larger town, but I was born here, like it here, and the job pays my mortgage and the rent on my office.

It was a sunny Monday morning in July. I was sorting through my files, wondering when my next client was going to walk through the door, when the phone rang. It was a man with a husky voice, and although his words were muffled, I could understand what he was saying.

"Thought you'd like to know. There are five bodies buried somewhere in town. All killed by the same hand."

I thought it was a crank call, and hung up.

The next morning, the first clue came in the mail. It was postmarked

"White River," typed on plain white paper. Bad spelling, and written in verse:

Five body's buried in White River. One mile south, too miles west. Take off you're shoes, but ware a vest.

It was at that point in time that I realized the guy was either demented, or there really were five bodies buried in White River, and that he expected me to play a game called "Follow the Clues."

I sat at my desk for a long time studying the note. What kind of a vest was he talking about? Suit vest? Body armor? A fishing vest? And one mile south from where? White River had a lot of streets heading south, and they all ended up at the river. That was when I realized I had to have a starting point, if I was going to play the game.

I closed up early, and stopped by the sheriff's department, hoping the sheriff could shed some light on my dilemma. Sheriff Black found it amaz-

ing that I'd actually been taken in by the prankster, and all but laughed me out of his office.

Suddenly hoping there were five bodies buried in White River, and that I could crack the case wide open, showing Mr. Big-shot Sheriff a thing or two, I drove back to the office, studied the map on the wall, and plotted out my route. I knew it might take four or five attempts, but sooner or later, I'd find the spot where I was supposed to take off my shoes, and wear a vest.

Emma concluded with, "I have a lot more of the story written, but it isn't polished, and I'm still working out the plot."

Judith cleared her throat. "Ah, well, what you read isn't exactly polished either, Emma. It is what I would call a first draft. You've given us the meat of the plot, but you've left out a good many elements. And where is your description? *Show* us the town and Jake Lamont. Make us *feel* his dilemma."

Orris spoke up. "River Road runs east

and west, so that means Jake has to head west along River Road. And no matter where he starts, it would still put him in the general vicinity of the Grange.''

''Not if he started west from Marshton Road,'' Nora Muller said. ''Two miles from that point would put him out near the Babkinses' farm.''

Nettie was bobbing her head. ''And the Babkinses' farm is right on West Willow Creek, where fishing is good. It's my guess Jake is supposed to wear a fishing vest, and wade in the creek. That's why he's supposed to take off his shoes.''

Lolly hugged the pink rabbit to her breast, and her dark eyes danced. ''Do you suppose the bodies are buried along the creek, or on old Babkins's property?''

''No way,'' Mrs. Wiggs announced. ''Emma said the bodies are buried in a rose garden, and you won't find one rose on the Babkinses' farm, or any other flowers, for that matter, because Rita Babkins has allergies. Even the smell of hay gets to her from time to time, if the wind is blowing in the right direction.''

Jennifer exchanged glances with Emma, and shook her head. She found it incredible that they were discussing Emma's story as though the crimes had actually been committed.

Emma waved a hand for attention. "Best you all remember that my story is only fiction, and *I'm* doing the writing. You want to know what happens? You are going to have to wait for the next installment."

"Heaven help us," Lenora muttered.

Mildred declared, "Well, *I* know why Emma didn't give us any descriptions. She was afraid we'd figure out who she's got a-playing the parts. Don't suppose it would matter much who she sees as Jake or the sheriff, but not one female resident in Calico would want to be cast as the killer."

Frustrated, Emma stuffed her papers into a folder, and sat down. "I guess everything I said to you fell on deaf ears. My story is fiction. My town is fictional. My characters are fictional."

Judith clapped her hands for attention. "I suggest we get to the real issue here, and that happens to be Emma's writing skills. Who can tell me what else is missing in Emma's story?''

"Dialogue," Tracy Madison said. "I wanted to hear the conversation between Jake and the sheriff."

Judith smiled. "That's very good, Tracy. Do you happen to have something to read that contains dialogue?"

Tracy was very blond, very pretty, and very arrogant. Her husband was a brilliant surgeon at the new hospital across White River Bridge, so Jennifer supposed that had something to do with her haughty attitude that seemed to say, "Look at me! I'm from a large city, my husband is a splendid surgeon, and I'm better than everybody. If you don't believe it, just ask me!" Nor was it a surprise that she'd set her story in a large hospital, and made the surgeon protagonist bigger than life.

Tracy stood up, and raised her chin. "As a matter of fact, I do." The room grew silent again, as Tracy began:

Dr. Peter Farnsworth removed his surgical gloves with a vociferous snap, tossed them in the refuse scuttle, and spoke to his esteemed colleague. "Job well done, John. The woman will walk again."

"Thanks to you, Peter," John said wearily. "That new procedure really works. Shall we go have a drink and celebrate?"

"Best you go without me," Peter said smilingly. "I have two more surgeries scheduled in the morning, and I must have adequate rest if I am to preform in my usual effulgent manner. But have a drink for me."

Judith's face had turned red, and she seemed to be having some difficulty breathing. Finally, she said, "Ah, well, you have a handle on dialogue okay, Tracy, but there are a few problems...."

Lolly spoke up. "I've just figured it out. Emma said that Jake was going to get a lot of clues. I'll bet he's going to find a clue when he gets to that spot where he's supposed to take off his shoes, and wear a vest."

"That's what I think," Orris said, looking down at the page of notes he'd written on Emma's story. "And I'll bet Jake ends up going around in circles for a long time before he receives the kinds of clues that will actually help him find the bodies."

Emma flushed. "You folks are being rude. We're supposed to be discussing Tracy's story."

"That's right, we are," Judith said, giving Emma an appreciative nod. "And I expect each and every one of you to give your fellow students the same kind of courtesy you would expect to receive."

Thoroughly chastised, the class settled down, but it was easy to see their minds weren't on Tracy or her badly written, tedious story. Every thought was on a detective named Jake Lamont, and his struggle to find five buried bodies somewhere in the fictitious town of White River, Nebraska.

"You should have seen it," Jennifer told her grandfather later that evening. "With the exception of Tracy Madison, Emma had everybody mesmerized. By the time class was over, even Judith was caught up in Emma's story, and admitted she couldn't wait for the next installment.''

''And from the looks of it,'' Wes said, ''Emma has every intention of coming through for them.'' He waved a hand at Emma's empty chair on the porch. ''Little did I know when I had that old typewriter repaired, that Emma would turn my study into an inner sanctum, and fill it with mystery and intrigue. And what's even more amazing, she does it all with just two fingers.''

Jennifer took a sip of her iced tea, and sighed. ''She's really enjoying it, Grandfather, but I can't help but look around and wonder how she can prefer to be in the house, when it's such a glorious evening. The honeysuckle is in bloom, and I can even smell the mint Emma planted under the kitchen window. It's a wonderful prelude to summer.''

Wes shrugged. ''Well, you know Emma, sweetheart. She never does anything halfway. She's been wanting to write a mystery story for a long time now, so best we let her get it out of her system."

"By the way, Ben called. Said he'll be at the clinic in the morning. They put him in a walking cast today, so he'll be able to get around a little easier. He admitted he's anxious to get back to work, and is rethinking his retirement date."

"He doesn't have a specific date."

"I think he's had one all along, only he's kept it to himself. But now that he's gotten a taste of the idle life, he's been forced to reconsider."

"Well, I hope he does," Jennifer said firmly. "Ben is a vital man, who is much too young to retire."

Wes took a sip of iced tea. "You mentioned Emma had everybody mesmerized except Tracy Madison. So, what was wrong with her?"

"I think she was jealous because Emma's story was getting all the attention. She'd written a piece about two doctors, and it was quite dreadful."

"So, was Emma's story worth all the attention?"

Jennifer gave her handsome, white-haired grandfather a fetching grin. "She hasn't told you about it?"

"Nope, and I've been afraid to ask. Heaven knows, I don't want to be the one to interfere with her creative genius."

"Well, it really is quite good. I don't know that much about writing, you understand, and according to Judith, Emma left out some important elements, but all in all, her plot is really compelling. The protagonist is a P.I. named Jake Lamont, who receives an anonymous phone call informing him that there are five bodies buried in town. Next, he gets a clue to their whereabouts and, from what I understand, it's the first of many clues, and each one will draw Jake closer to the bodies, and I assume, the murderer."

"Boy, oh boy," Wes said. "I had no idea she was writing about murder and mayhem. But I guess I should have expected it, because that's what she likes to read. I think she's read Paul Stanford's book, ummm, what's the title?"

"The Headless Horseman of Bayberry Street."

"Uh-huh, well, she's read it at least four times."

A few minutes later, Emma padded out on the porch, with a pencil behind her ear and a scowl on her face. "What's another word for 'dynamic'?" she asked, sitting down in her chair.

Wes grinned. "Energetic, aggressive, maybe powerful. But if you're trying to describe your detective, what's wrong with dynamic?"

Emma eyed Wes intently. "So, Jennifer told you about Jake, did she? Did she tell you about the plot?"

"She did. Hey, if you can read your story to your class, why should I get left out?"

Emma lowered her eyes. "I didn't tell you about him, or the plot, because I thought you might try to talk me into writing something a little less gruesome. You know, like about an old lady who dies and leaves all her money to her cat."

Wes said, "And then the whole family

fights over the cat? I think I've read that one before, Emma, and believe me, originality counts for something. Your plot sounds fresh and original. Good going. I'm proud of you.''

Emma flushed rosy pink, and the corners of her mouth dimpled. "That was a very nice thing to say, Wes, even though I don't deserve it. Judith says my writing lacks description, so that's what I'm doing now. I'm going over the first few pages, and filling them up with description."

"I wouldn't go overboard," Jennifer said. "I rather like your straightforward style of writing. But if you want a good word to describe Jake, how about 'charismatic'?"

Emma beamed. "That's perfect!"

"Okay, so now you've got the right word, so how about a glass of iced tea to celebrate?" Wes said.

Emma's eyes settled on the pitcher of iced tea, and the smile turned into a frown. "Who made the tea?" she asked.

"I did," Wes said.

She harrumphed. "And I'll bet you added at least five pounds of sugar."

"The only thing in the tea is a little lemon, because I thought you'd be joining us on this splendid spring night, and I know how you feel about sugar."

Emma looked out over the moon-splashed garden, and sighed. "It is lovely tonight, isn't it? Well, I'm afraid I can't take the time to enjoy it, or much of anything, until I finish my story, so I'd better get back to work. This is Thursday, and that only gives me five days to finish and polish the next installment."

It was Wes's turn to sigh. "They aren't going to tar and feather you if it isn't written, Emma."

"I wouldn't be too sure about that," Jennifer said, after Emma went in the house. "If you'd been there tonight, you'd understand. Emma has a captive audience.

"Now I think I'll turn in. It's been a long day."

"Ummm, did Emma say how long this story is going to be?"

Jennifer could see the loneliness in his

blue eyes, and knew exactly what he was feeling. Emma was much more than a housekeeper. She was his best friend, and he missed the closeness they'd always shared. Especially on special nights like this. She gave him a hug. "No, she didn't, but I wouldn't worry too much about it. The class is only six weeks long, so we only have four more weeks to go."

"A month," he said dismally. "We'll be well into summer by then. Well, let's hope by that time she remembers my name." He managed a smile. "Guess I'm just feeling a little sorry for myself, and maybe a little guilty, too. Or maybe I'm just spoiled. She's been so much a part of my life for so long, and at my age, it's hard to accept changes."

"You're making it sound as though Emma is going to become a famous author, and walk out of our lives," Jennifer admonished.

Wes shrugged. "Stranger things have happened. Sleep tight, sweetheart. I'll see you in the morning."

"Are you going to bed now?"

"Not yet. I'm going to the chapel, and have a little talk with God. Maybe he can set me straight."

Wishing she could say something to help her grandfather get over the mood that was so unlike him, Jennifer climbed the stairs, and listened to the clickety-clack of the typewriter keys.

With a sigh, she headed for her bedroom. It had been a long day, but she had the feeling it was going to be an even longer weekend.

Chapter Two

"So, you're not looking forward to the weekend, huh?" Ben said, putting the CLOSED sign on the front door.

"Would you, under the circumstances?" Jennifer asked, straightening up the magazines in the waiting room. "You've been here most of the afternoon. You've heard the one hundred and one questions I've had to answer."

"Yeah, well, better you than me, kiddo. I was all prepared to answer one hundred and one questions about my accident, even though it's old news by now. I guess there

The Pink Rabbit Caper

is something about seeing a cast on a grown man's leg that brings out a perverse curiosity in people, and it isn't enough to know I fell down the basement steps. Oh, no. They want to know *how* I fell down the steps, and why. So I tell them I was carrying a box and missed the first step, and they think, 'Sure, right. Why don't you tell us the truth, old man? You had a few tee many martoonies, or your wife pushed you, or you had a dizzy spell. Come on, 'fess up!' "

Jennifer tried for a smile. "Well, unfortunately, I think it's a little more than perverse curiosity when it comes to Emma's writing. When I went home for lunch, Grandfather said the phone had been ringing off the hook all morning, and the calls weren't only from members of our writing class. Apparently word has gotten around about Emma's mystery story, and everybody wants to make suggestions on how to write it, or how they think it should end."

Ben shook his head. "It's strange the way people can get involved, even when it isn't any of their business. Take the mailman. He delivered the hospital bill the other day, and he stood right there on the stoop, expecting me to open it in front of him.

"Seriously, it's good to be back, Jennifer. I think even Pansy missed me. You see the way she's been following me around all afternoon?"

Ben was a tall, rugged-looking man in his mid-sixties, with a teasing manner, and a warm smile. And his eyes were full of mischief now. Pansy was a cream-colored potbellied pig they had adopted as the clinic's resident pet after the owner died, and although she had a special enclosure, she also had the run of the clinic, as long as they didn't have any patients. Though "run" really wasn't the appropriate word. At the moment, Pansy was in Ben's office, snoozing under his desk.

"She missed the dried kernels of corn you always carry around in your lab coat pocket," Jennifer returned. "Seriously, we've all missed you. Tina was saying just the other day how much she missed your wonderful smile and silly 'knock, knock' jokes.''

Ben looked at his watch. "Speaking of Tina, shouldn't she be here by now?"

"She said she might be late because of finals. It's hard to believe she'll be graduating in a couple of weeks."

Ben sighed. "Or that she'll be going off to college in the fall. Now, that's a young lady who is going to be sorely missed."

"I know, and sooner or later, we'll have to think about getting a replacement. And finding somebody with Tina's enthusiasm for veterinary medicine, and her marvelous way with animals, is going to be next impossible."

"Uh-huh, especially when you add in the fact she's one heck of a hard worker. I was thinking maybe we should put an ad in the paper now, and if we get lucky and find somebody we think will work out, then he or she could spend the summer working with Tina. It would be sort of a training program."

"That's a terrific idea, Ben, and then we could—" Jennifer broke off, and frowned.

"A car just pulled up out front, but it isn't Tina."

Ben opened the door. "It's Barbara Thurman and her Maltese... No, it isn't Fancy Dancer. It looks like a Maltese puppy... Oh-oh. It doesn't look good, and Barbara is crying."

Jennifer hurried out the door to help the woman, and the sight of the limp puppy twisted her heart.

"Help her, please!" Barbara Thurman cried, handing Jennifer the puppy. "She was having some sort of a fit, and then just fell over. I thought she was dead, but then realized she was breathing...."

Tears again, and while Ben tried to console the nearly hysterical woman, Jennifer rushed the puppy into the emergency examining room.

"What was she doing just before she had the convulsion?" Jennifer asked, quickly examining the tiny lump of white fur, which looked outrageously small on the large metal table.

Barbara Thurman, who was married to Ray Thurman—the *other* judge in town—

was a tall, handsome woman with dark hair and eyes. She also had a habit of going into a panic if Fancy Dancer so much as sneezed, but this wasn't a false alarm today. The puppy was in serious trouble.

Barbara stood in the doorway, trembling and stammering. "I-I don't know, exactly. I-I was in the kitchen getting a roast ready to put in the oven, and Lily was playing with Fancy. Yes, they were playing on the terrace. I-I remembering looking out the window and thinking how great it was they were actually getting along. My husband was against getting the puppy. He said because Fancy was getting on in years, he was afraid a puppy would be too much for her. And now this . . ."

"Whoa," Tina said, hurrying into the room. "I saw the car, and thought you might have an emergency."

"The puppy is in shock," Jennifer said. "Ben, get me some sugar water and brandy, and Tina, get a warming bed ready." To Barbara Thurman, she said, "I believe the puppy is suffering from Von Gierke syndrome. I know, that sounds scary, and I won't lie to you, it can be fatal. But I think you got her here in time. It's a condition we encounter in toy breeds, especially in Chihuahuas, Yorkies, and Maltese, and always in puppies. The onset is characterized by sudden coma, shock, and occasionally convulsions. We don't know why this happens, but several things can be a contributing factor, and exhaustion is one of them. If Lily was playing hard just before it happened, that would be my guess.''

Ben handed Jennifer a syringe filled with sugar water that had a tube attached to the end in place of the needle.

Jennifer took the syringe and placed the tube in the puppy's mouth. ''Though I'm only going to give her just a few drops at a time, it's imperative she take most of this. Her blood sugar has been lowered, causing hypoglycemia. I'll also give her a little brandy as a stimulant, and when she rallies, we'll put her on the warming bed. If we're in the time, she'll come out of it soon. We could give her an injection, but I prefer to do it this way if at all possible.

"Ben, why don't you take Mrs. Thurman

to the waiting room, so she can sit down. And you'd better sit down, too. You've been on your leg far too much today."

Barbara groaned. "I forgot all about your leg, Ben. I'm sorry to be causing all this trouble."

After they left the room, Tina lowered her voice and said, "Is the condition more serious than you were letting on? I mean, is the puppy going to die?"

Jennifer looked into Tina's caring brown eyes, and smiled. "I think she's going to be just fine, honey. Look, she's already coming around."

Ten minutes later, the puppy began whining and wiggling to get up, and while Tina put her on the warming bed, Jennifer went into the waiting room, to tell Barbara Thurman the good news. And give her instructions. "If this ever happens again, I want you to call us, and then try to correct the problem yourself, because just the length of time it takes for you to get to town, or for us to get to your house, might make the difference between life and death. Use an eyedropper or a spoon, and either sugar water or any form of syrup. Even molasses, if you have it. Also, a bit of brandy as a stimulant is advisable."

"Will I be able to take her home today?"

"Absolutely. We'll only keep her on the warming bed for ten or fifteen minutes, and Tina is keeping an eye on her. In the meantime, I think you could use a cup of coffee."

"I'll get it," Ben said, heading for the office.

Barbara sighed. "Life can be so difficult. One minute everything is fine, and then . . . Ben is a good example. There he was, carrying a box down to the basement, and the next thing you know, he's at the bottom of the stairs with a broken leg. One minute Lily and Fancy were playing, and then . . ." She closed her eyes, and shuddered. "You tell Emma I think she's doing the right thing, writing that book. Everybody had better do what they want to do today, because tomorrow, it might be too late."

Ben had returned with the coffee, and

raised a brow. "How did you find out about Emma's book?"

"Judith Stoker called me this morning."

"Emma isn't writing a book," Jennifer said, thinking about all the other phone calls that had probably been made during the course of the day. "It's a story."

Barbara shrugged. "Book or story, the point is, Emma is doing something she really wants to do. I say, good for her!" And then a flush touched her cheeks. "Is it true she's setting the story in Calico, and that the cast of characters will be real Calico residents?"

Slightly irritated, Jennifer said, "Emma's town and characters are fictitious, Mrs. Thurman. No matter what you've heard."

"Uh-huh, well, I've heard that's what she *wants* everybody to think. My husband says she'd better be careful, or she could end up getting sued. Of course, you're good friends with Willy Ashton, and I'm sure he's giving Emma good legal advice. Oh, I know he's the mayor now, but he's still a lawyer. Hmmm. You're good friends with Ken Hering, too, and he's a reporter. Maybe you'd better watch what you say when you're around him. I'm not telling you what to do, of course, but..."

By the time Barbara Thurman left with the puppy, Jennifer had the beginning of a clawing kind of headache. And it was worse knowing that it probably wasn't going to be any better at home.

It was after five when Jennifer walked into the kitchen, and what she found brought on an audible gasp. She'd expected it to be bad, but nothing like this! "What on earth..."

Wes waved a spoon. "Don't ask. It's been one of those days, Jennifer, and right about now, I'm ready to throw the whole mess down the sink, and order a pizza."

Jennifer looked around at the dirty dishes on the counters and in the sink, the pots bubbling over on the stove, and her grandfather's flustered face, and simply couldn't imagine what could have caused all this chaos. It was true he didn't do much cooking, because the kitchen was usually

Emma's domain, but when he did, he always kept things neat. "Clean up as you go," that was his motto.

"What happened to 'clean up as you go?'" Jennifer asked, turning down the burners under the pots.

Just then the phone rang, and Wes muttered, "That's what's been happening. I've burned up two pans of pasta answering that blasted phone, and burned a batch of spaghetti sauce, too." He picked up the receiver, and barked out, "Hello!" And then, "Hang on, let me find you on the list. Okay, I've got you. Uh-huh . . ."

Wes was writing something down on a sheet of paper while he listened to the caller. Finally, he grumbled, "I've got it. Have a good day, Penelope."

He hung up and waved a hand at the stack of papers on the table. "You see all that? Messages for Emma. Six sheets so far, and counting. That last call was from Penelope Davis. At first I was just taking the messages down randomly, but then I started getting return calls, where the caller wanted me to read back what they'd said the first time. That's when I began numbering the calls. Quick reference.''

"Why don't you just let the phone ring?" Jennifer asked incredulously.

"I tried that, but Emma had a fit. Said the ringing phone was interfering with her concentration. I thought about unplugging it, but a couple of callers said if I didn't take down their messages, they were coming over. Well, the last thing I need is a house full of folks all clamoring with bright ideas. Not that I haven't had a few pop in. But most of it has been over the phone." Wes looked at the pasta in the pan, and sighed. "Looks like I'll make it this time."

Jennifer put on an apron, ran hot water in the sink, and added a squirt of detergent. "Does Emma know what's going on out here?"

"You mean the phone calls?"

"No, I mean the mess you've made *because* of the phone calls."

"Ha! You've got to be kidding. She hasn't poked her nose out of the study all day. I took her a sandwich and a cup of tea at noon, and she didn't touch any of it.

Worse, she's using three fingers to type, and that's scary. Who knows what will happen if she learns how to use all her fingers. You sit down and relax, and let me do that. I know you've had a rough day at the clinic."

Wes was wearing jeans and a plaid shirt. He'd rolled up the sleeves, but one cuff had fallen down, and was now below dishwater level. Jennifer waved him off. "Go change your shirt, Grandfather, and then I want *you* to sit down and relax. No ifs or buts!"

Wes looked down at the wet shirtsleeve like it was a foreign entity, and sighed. "Well, don't worry about answering the phone. If it rings, I'll take it upstairs."

Ten minutes later, Wes returned to the kitchen, wearing a blue polo shirt, and a smug look on his face. "Ten whole minutes, and no calls."

"It's the dinner hour," Jennifer said, wiping off the table. "We should be safe for an hour or two. I made a pot of coffee. Pour me a cup, too?"

Wes poured two cups of coffee, and

sniffed the air appreciatively. "The spaghetti sauce smells good."

"Just opened a jar, and added some spices. Is there a reason why we're fixing spaghetti when Emma detests it?"

Wes's mouth drooped down. "Figured she isn't going to join us, so might as well fix what I like. Well, that didn't come out sounding right. Most of the time, she fixes everything I like."

"And if she decides to join us?"

"Then she can open a can of soup. I'm sorry if I'm not sounding particularly charitable, sweetheart, but this whole thing is really beginning to get to me. I'm concerned about her, too. She can't go on day after day without eating. It's like she's in some sort of a frenzy, and can't find her way out."

"Sounds like she has the town whipped into a frenzy, too. I read some of those suggestions while you were upstairs. But what really intrigued me were those callers who stated, in no uncertain terms, that Emma should forget the whole project, because all she's going to do is stir up trouble."

Wes sat down at the table. "I only had two or three like that, and not one of them would give me a name. Nor did I recognize their voices. Sure makes you wonder how many skeletons are rattling around in Calico's closets."

"I know, but you want to know what really amazes me? Everybody thinks Emma is actually going to write about them. I swear, Grandfather, I don't think they know what fiction is."

"I don't know if it's that so much, or the fact they're afraid that Emma is going to turn her story into one of those exposé books, where even though the names have been changed, everybody knows who they are supposed to be. And that takes us right back to the skeletons in the closet."

Jennifer began chopping tomatoes and cucumbers for the tossed salad as she thought about that. Finally, she said, "So who do you think would be the most likely candidate to have a skeleton or two in their closet?"

"Elmer Dodd, for one. He's keeping a low profile since he lost the election to

Willy, but I've heard he's been having some clandestine meetings with Ed Dunn out at Boodie's Roadhouse, so who knows what he's got up his sleeve."

"Ed Dunn is the town realtor. Maybe Elmer is trying to buy up more property?"

"Maybe. But rumor has it the dairy is losing money."

Jennifer gave Wes a sly wink. "What about Norman Fuller? Nettie lives next door to him, and you know what she says."

Wes grinned. "Uh-huh. He looks like Anthony Perkins and she hasn't seen his wife in years, so she figures he has her stashed away in a room somewhere, living on bread and water."

"Nettie thinks he looks like Anthony Perkins playing the part of Norman Bates, and that's even scarier." Jennifer sighed. "Do you want me to try to talk to Emma? Maybe try to make her understand that she isn't doing our nerves, or her health, any good, carrying on like this?"

"You can try, sweetheart, but I have my doubts she'll listen."

"Listen to what?" Emma said, trudging

The Pink Rabbit Caper 47

into the kitchen. She looked at the spaghetti sauce in the pan, and made a face. "Whose idea was *that?*"

Wes cleared his throat. "Were you planning on cooking supper?"

"To tell you the truth, I haven't even thought about supper. Well, don't worry about me. I'll eat something later."

"But we *are* worried about you," Jennifer said gently. "Grandfather says you haven't eaten all day; you're still in your housecoat, so you tell us. I'll bet even Stephen King takes the time to eat."

Emma sat down at the table, and ran a hand over her eyes. "I've hit a rough spot in my story, that's all."

"Writer's block?" Wes asked.

"No, not that. But I've only managed to get one page written all afternoon."

Jennifer said, "So, I would think that this is the perfect time to take a break. Why don't you go freshen up, and I'll fix you an omelet and some toast."

Emma opened her mouth to reply, and then frowned. "What's all that?"

She was referring to the stack of messages, and Wes sighed. "Phone messages. Mostly suggestions regarding your story. It seems like the whole town wants to help you write it."

"Throw them out," Emma said flatly. "This is *my* story, and I'm the one who is going to write it." She gave Jennifer a wan smile. "I'll go freshen up now, but I don't want you to bother fixing me an omelet. I'll have a little bit of spaghetti and some salad. Maybe a cup of tea." She looked around. "You know, I was feeling a mite guilty about shirking my duties, but I should have known I was worrying needlessly." She patted Jennifer's hand. "Your granddaddy is a wonder. He managed to fix supper without one splatter or spill."

"Why didn't you tell her?" Jennifer whispered, after Emma left the kitchen.

"Why didn't *you* tell her?" Wes whispered back.

Chapter Three

Because Ben was spending more and more time at the clinic, and getting around quite well on his walking cast, Jennifer gratefully accepted his suggestion that she take Tuesday and Wednesday off. The last four days had been crammed full of uninvited visitors and phone calls, and she was exhausted, for one thing. But more importantly, her grandfather was beginning to wear down, too, and they couldn't put it off any longer. They had to talk to Emma, and somehow make her understand that with their busy schedules, there was no way they could keep on top of the things that had to be done around the house, and run interference while Emma finished her story. And that left two choices. Either they were going to have to let things slide, or hire temporary help. There was a third choice, of course, that Emma simply stop writing, or at least slow down, but just the *thought* of mentioning it to her gave them the jeebies.

So now it was late Tuesday afternoon, class would be starting in two hours, and they were no closer to having "that talk" with Emma than before. But there was one plus in their topsy-turvy existence. The phone hadn't rung all afternoon, and the silence was wonderful.

"Can't bother her now," Wes said, getting a chicken casserole out of the freezer. "She's finally worked through her problems, and the pages are beginning to stack up. The way I see it, the sooner she can type 'The End' on the last page, the sooner things can get back to normal." He grimaced. "Now, if I could just get over feeling guilty...."

Jennifer finished setting the table, and frowned. "Why should you feel guilty?"

Wes sighed. "Emma has been our housekeeper for a good many years, but she's also a part of the family. This is her home, and it just seems to me we've taken her for granted. She does the housecleaning, the cooking, and the laundry because she's expected to, and now, just because she wants to take a couple of weeks off to write a story, everything falls apart. I think we should be handling it better, that's all."

"I agree, but we're not the only ones to blame, Grandfather. Emma has definitely gone overboard, and that's not our fault. All things in moderation, isn't that what you're always preaching?"

"Yes, but how can you apply that to creativity, or the simple love of something? Emma is a passionate, determined woman, and no matter what she's doing, she isn't going to do it halfway. That word just isn't in her vocabulary, and that's what makes her so unique. And it's one of the reasons why we love her so much. Ahem, I've come to a decision, sweetheart. I'm going to hire temporary help. Having somebody here a few hours a day will take the pressure off everybody, and it will make life a whole lot easier.

"By the way, I've decided to tag along tonight. Just as an observer, of course."

"I think that's a grand idea, Grandfather, but I don't know about hiring temporary help. Somehow, I don't think Emma is going to like the idea of having a stranger in the house."

"Well then, we'll just have to make her understand, that's all."

"And when do you propose to do that?"

"Tonight, after we get home. And it doesn't necessarily have to be a stranger. The economy is tight right now, and there are a lot of folks around town looking for ways to make an extra dollar."

Jennifer was about to tell him she had the feeling it was going to be a lot easier said than done, but Emma had walked into the kitchen, and her beautiful face was aglow.

"Finally finished the scene I'm going to read tonight, and I think Judith is going to

The Pink Rabbit Caper 53

be very pleased." She peered in the oven at the casserole, nodded her head in approval, and gave Wes a dimpled grin. "Why don't you come along with us tonight, Wes? That way, you can hear my story firsthand."

"I'd be delighted," Wes said, giving Jennifer a wink that clearly said everything was going to be just dandy, because Emma was in a good mood.

Wishing she had her grandfather's confidence, Jennifer opened a can of green beans, and could only pray Emma's good mood continued, and that the evening went well.

But when they pulled into the parking lot at a little before seven, and they couldn't find a place to park, Jennifer had the first clue things weren't going to go well at all.

"It looks like the senior citizens are having some sort of a meeting," Emma said with a frown, "and that seems mighty strange. Nobody mentioned it to me. And isn't that Ken Hering's Bronco? What on earth is he doing here?"

It was indeed Ken Hering's Bronco, and

Jennifer's apprehension grew. Ken was a good friend, but he was also a reporter for *The Calico Review*. Nor had she heard anything about the seniors having a meeting, and moreover, they had promised they wouldn't schedule any events on Tuesday and Thursday nights, so the students in the writing class would be able to park closer to the building. Now, because of the sea of vehicles, Wes had to park in the second lot, which meant they would have a healthy hike around the duck pond and through the rose gardens.

Because of it, Wes let them out near the entrance to the front walkway, and said he'd meet them inside.

"Your granddaddy is always so thoughtful," Emma said, smoothing down her new flowered dress. "Why don't we just wait for him here. It isn't seven yet, and who cares if we're a little late? What is Judith going to do, expel us?"

Emma's little stab at humor put a smile on her face, but not on Jennifer's, because she had suddenly realized the recreation room, though lit up, was empty. Other than the recreation room, there were two meeting rooms, separated by an accordion-pleated partition. The writing class was only using one side, and there was no way the other side could accommodate the drivers of all those vehicles in the parking lot. Waves of apprehension washed over her, because the only other room in the building was the kitchen, and it wasn't likely they were holding a meeting in there. Fortunately, Emma was standing with her back to the building, and hadn't noticed the peculiar situation.

But Jennifer could see the concern in Wes's eyes when he joined them a few minutes later, and she knew what he was thinking. Was it possible everybody had come to hear Emma read her story? Was that why the phone had been silent all afternoon? Had they been making secret little calls to one another, planning a mass invasion?

Jennifer felt a little light-headed just thinking about it, and when they reached the entrance, she held out a hand. "I-I think we'd better consider something before we go in . . ." She took a deep breath. "In case you haven't noticed, nobody is in the rec room, and there are at least three dozen cars in the parking lot. Well, they aren't meeting in the kitchen, so that means they are either all stuffed into the room next to ours, or . . ."

Wes muttered, "Or, they slid back the partition to make one big meeting room, and that's where they are, waiting to hear Emma read her story."

Emma touched Wes's arm, and smiled. "Relax, Wes. First of all, I don't believe for one minute all those folks are here to hear my little story. But if by chance, they are, I think it's quite lovely of them."

Wes groaned. "Are you forgetting about how upset you were with all those phone calls, and uninvited guests?"

"That was because they were trying to tell me how to write my story, and they were interfering with my concentration. Now it doesn't matter. I know exactly what I'm going to write, and how to write it, and I wouldn't mind one bit if I had an audience."

The Pink Rabbit Caper

They were walking along the hallway now, and Jennifer could only stare at the crowd spilling out from the meeting room. Somebody yelled, "Here they come!" And that was followed by a scramble of feet.

Emma led the way through the crowd, and held her head high, nodding and smiling at all the familiar faces. Penelope Davis, a widow with fifteen cats. Emily Wilcox, busybody. Eighty-year-old Doc Chambers. Sally, a waitress at the coffee shop. John Wexler, Jr., editor of *The Calico Review*. Martha Brown, the hairdresser. Barbara Thurman, judge's wife. Pete Nelson, barber. Jasper Willis, who owned the janitorial service in town, and his wife. Rose Kelly, who owned the rooming house. Joshua Miller, candy-store owner, and his wife. Mary Ellis, grocery checker. Annie, the florist. Portias Landers, dentist, and the Cramers, who owned a farm east of town. There were a few people Jennifer didn't know, and of course all the students taking the writing class, who looked as flustered and miserable as Jennifer felt.

And then Ken Hering was beside her,

giving her a comforting hug. "I thought you guys knew all about this until I saw Judith trying to kick everybody out. What a muddle that was! And there was nothing she could do or say to convince them that they shouldn't be here to hear Emma read her story. And then when she saw my camera... Well, let's just say I was in great fear of receiving bodily damage. Fortunately, John, Jr., was able to calm her down."

"How did you hear about it?" Jennifer asked, reaching up to straighten Ken's tie.

Ken ran a hand through his red hair. "Guess my hair is standing on end, too, huh? That shows you how physical things were getting. I found out by way of an anonymous caller, who told me Emma had written a best-seller, and if I wanted to get a newsworthy story firsthand, I'd better be here tonight. That was about four this afternoon. I was going to call you for verification, but then I had to go out to the mall. Somebody set off the overhead sprinkler system in the department store, and it was quite a mess."

"And so is this," Jennifer said dejectedly. "And what really kills me, it doesn't seem to be bothering Emma at all. Look at her. She's all smiles and handshakes."

Ken nodded. "She looks pretty terrific. Is that a new dress?"

"Yes, it is. It's almost like she knew this was going to happen, and dressed accordingly."

"Uh-huh, well, your grandfather sure doesn't look very happy about it."

Jennifer was going to tell Ken how chaotic the last few days had been, but Judith was demanding attention, and she wasn't going to be ignored.

"Please, everybody. If you'll be quiet, I'd like to get on with this! Either find a chair and sit down, or stand against the back wall." She waited a few minutes while the people tried to oblige, and then went on. "I'm going to say this only once. This is a class for beginning writers. We are in our third week now, with only three more weeks to go. That doesn't give us a lot of time, and confusion like this is only going to set us back." She looked at

Emma. "I'll leave this up to you, Emma. It seems these 'considerate' people are here tonight to hear your story, and I'm not going to try to reason why. I'm simply going to ask you how you want to handle it. If you don't want to read in front of all these people, or if you want to go home, I'll certainly understand."

When groans of protest erupted around the room, Emma raised a hand. "I don't mind reading in front of these fine folks, but I think it should be left up to the other students, Judith. I'll admit, I'm flattered by all the attention, but this is a writing class after all, and I agree it's being disrupted. If I leave, maybe the crowd will leave, and then the rest of you can get down to business." She looked around at the students, and all of them were shaking their heads.

But it was Lolly Peabody who spoke up. "I've spent the last five days eagerly waiting to hear your next installment, Emma. And I'm sure I speak for the rest of us."

"Is that lady for real?" Ken whispered in Jennifer's ear. "I've seen her around town, carrying that pink bunny, but I always thought she was taking it to a kid. You know, like maybe a grandchild. Didn't realize she wears false eyelashes, either. Whoa. Must be two inches long."

Jennifer grinned, and whispered back, "She's for real. I think she thinks she's a flapper."

"Uh-huh, right out of the Roaring Twenties."

Lolly was wearing a bright red dress with lots of tassels and fringe, and she actually looked rather attractive, if you could get beyond the bizarreness of her outfit.

Meg Ashton was speaking. "Well, I agree with Lolly. Emma's story is all I've been thinking about, too. Let's give this night to Emma, and maybe her creativity will give us all the incentive to get down to work, and accomplish something ourselves."

Emma looked at Tracy Madison. "And what about you, Tracy? How do you feel?"

Tracy lifted her chin saucily. "I'll agree to it, but only if I can have equal time. Maybe the rest of you have wasted your time thinking about Emma's story, but I haven't. I've spent the last five days at my computer, and the words have simply spewed forth.''

"You have as much right to read your story as I do," Emma said sweetly. "What about you, Lenora? As I recall, you weren't too happy about my subject matter."

Lenora Hyde waved her infamous pink hanky. "Let's just get on with it, so I can get some air. I have a touch of claustrophobia, you know, and with so many people in the room, I can scarcely breathe!"

John, Jr., with every hair on his blond head in place, and impeccably dressed as usual, stepped forward. "We're going to serve refreshments in the recreation room when we're through here. Courtesy of *The Calico Review,* of course. At that time, I'd like to interview you, Emma, and of course Ken Hering and I will be taking some photos for the morning edition. All with your permission, of course, Emma."

Emma smiled. "I don't mind at all, John, Jr. Now, best we get on with this, before Lenora faints dead away."

Judith cleared her throat. "Well, I guess,

for fear if we don't it's likely to cause a lynching, we'll begin with you, Emma.''

Suddenly feeling a little claustrophobic herself, Jennifer said, "I have to get some air, Ken..."

Ken needed no further prompting. He took her arm, and escorted her out of the room. And they didn't stop until they were in the little courtyard at the rear of the building, where floodlights lit up the night. Spring flowers in planter boxes spilled over everywhere, and their sweet scent wafted through the air.

Ken waited until they were seated on a bench before he said, "Isn't Emma going to be upset with you for leaving?"

Jennifer sighed. "She'll never miss me, Ken. She has her fan club, and seems to be loving every minute of it. Besides, I can read her story anytime I want. All I have to do is ask."

"And have you read it?"

"No, but I heard the first installment last Thursday night in class. It was quite good, actually, but I have to tell you, she isn't Ed McBain, Robert Parker, or Paul Stanford, yet it's hard to believe she isn't, the way people are acting. The phone rang nonstop all weekend long. People wanting to give Emma ideas for the story."

"And did she use their ideas?"

"No, and she wouldn't talk to them, either. Grandfather and I had to run interference, because she wouldn't come out of the study. She barely took the time to eat."

"It sounds like she's determined. So, what's the story about?"

Jennifer told him, and sighed. "Shouldn't you be inside, taking pictures of our illustrious celebrity?"

"If John, Jr., wants photos, he can handle it. I'd rather be here with you. You sound exhausted, Jennifer. And maybe even a little disturbed. You know I'm a good listener, if you want to talk about it."

"To tell you the truth, I don't know what I feel, Ken. I love Emma with all my heart, yet now I'm beginning to wonder if I know her at all. Nothing seems to matter to her anymore except her writing."

Ken grinned. "Didn't you know all writers are supposed to be a little nuts?"

The Pink Rabbit Caper 65

Jennifer gave him a wan smile. "Does that include journalists?"

"Absolutely. May I make a suggestion? Relax with this, Jennifer, and be happy for Emma. She's wanted to write a mystery for a long time, and not too many people get the chance to realize their dream."

Jennifer lowered her head. "Now you're making me feel guilty."

He kissed her cheek. "That wasn't my intention. It looks like Emma has finished reading. Here comes your grandfather, and this time, he's smiling."

"The lady has talent," Wes said, joining them on the bench. "You could've heard a pin drop while she was reading. Not that she read all that much. Just enough to whet their appetites. Now she's answering questions, because everybody wants to know what's going to happen next."

"Did Jake Lamont find the spot where he was supposed to take off his shoes and wear a vest?"

"He did. It was a creek east of town. The second clue was nailed to a tree on the other side. Said for him to hike the creek east to the bend, and then fill the pockets of the fishing vest full of pebbles.''

Jennifer shook her head. "Do I dare ask why?"

"Because from there, he was supposed to cut directly across Farmer John's cornfield, and head for the pond, and he would need the rocks to throw at Farmer John's nasty geese if he expected to get through."

"And?"

"That's where she left it. Oh, and are you ready for this? John, Jr., wants to print her story in the newspaper. From the beginning, and one installment every couple of days. That way, the town can be kept up-to-date. He sounded as though he intends to give her some money, too. Needless to say, Emma was delighted, along with about everybody in the room."

"Do you think Emma can keep up with that kind of a schedule?" Jennifer asked.

Wes shrugged. "Only time will tell, but Emma didn't seem too concerned. By the way, I was talking to Rose Kelly, and she said her widowed aunt is in town, and plans to stay the summer. Said she might be interested in some temporary work. Guess she's had it pretty hard since her husband died. Rose said she'll have her aunt call me in the morning."

Ken whistled through his teeth. "Are you guys actually considering hiring somebody to do Emma's job, while she writes her story?"

"That's exactly what we're going to do," Wes said. "Jennifer and I have tried to keep things up around the house, but with our busy schedules, it's almost impossible. Now with Emma working on deadlines for the newspaper, it will be even worse."

"And Emma doesn't mind?" Ken asked.

"Emma doesn't know about it yet," Jennifer said. "And yes, I think she's going to mind. To tell you the truth, I think she's going to have a fit."

Wes got to his feet. "Well, you're going to be pleasantly surprised, sweetheart. Emma knows about it. She was right there when I was talking to Rose Kelly, and she didn't bat an eyelash. Just said she thought it was a good idea, and that it would make things easier on all of us.

"Shall we join the crowd in the rec room? I heard they're serving chocolate cake and punch, and not knowing how long it's going to be before Emma bakes another cake..."

He looked away, but not before Jennifer saw the sadness in his eyes. Their life was in for some big changes, and there was nothing they could do about it.

The next morning, Jennifer awoke to bright sunlight, the sound of voices, the clack of typewriter keys, and a pounding headache. She'd overslept, after spending a good portion of the night tossing and turning, and wasn't in the mood for company. But the coffee was downstairs, and for just one cup, she was willing to face all manner of visitors, welcome or not.

Wearing jeans and a gray sweatshirt, Jennifer groggily made her way downstairs, and had just reached the foyer when she realized her grandfather was in the kitchen, laughing. It was a warm, rich, wonderful sound that she hadn't heard in days. Unwelcome visitor or not, the person had certainly brightened his morning.

"Ah, here she is now!" Wes said, getting up from the kitchen table. "Sweetheart, this is Gloria Anderson, Rose Kelly's aunt. Gloria, this is my granddaughter, Jennifer."

Jennifer shook the woman's hand, and found herself staring. Dark curly hair and deep, sea green eyes. Small, trim figure under tan slacks and a white blouse, and an absolutely gorgeous face. Pert nose, high cheekbones, and flawless skin. Age? Maybe forty-five or fifty.

"Hello, Jennifer," Gloria drawled. "Your grandfather was just telling me about all the wonderful work you do at the clinic."

"Do you like animals?" Jennifer asked, pouring herself a cup of coffee.

"Oh, my, yes. When my Alan was alive, we always had a pet of some sort. He liked dogs, and I was partial to cats, so we usually had one of each. Now I move around so much, having a pet is out of the question." She gave a wistful little sigh. "Maybe someday I'll settle down again, and things will be different."

"Where are you from?" Jennifer asked.

"Originally? California. After Alan died, I went to stay with my daughter in Chicago, then it was on to Detroit. I have a son living in Detroit, but he has such a large family...." She sighed again. "I'll be honest, Jennifer. Since my husband died, things haven't been all that great financially. Alan was a love, but he wasn't very good with money. He made a lot of bad investments, and it took just about every cent to pay the bills. Unfortunately, I'm one of those women who made a career out of being a wife and mother, so I never learned to do anything else. But I don't want to be a burden, and that's why this job is so important. My niece is letting me stay in the rooming house, but I want to pay my way while I'm here. Eventually, I hope to find a full-time job. Maybe even go back to school."

Wes cleared his throat. "Ah, well, I told Gloria the job is hers if she wants it."

Gloria smiled. "I know it's only a few hours a day, but every little bit will help." She looked around the kitchen. "This is such a wonderful house. . . . Well, I can't wait to get started."

"So, when will you be starting?" Jennifer asked.

"Right now. Your grandfather was just going over the things that need to be done."

Jennifer looked at Wes. "Have you told Emma about this, Grandfather?"

"Uh-huh. I introduced her to Gloria, and then had to apologize to Gloria in the next breath, and explain, because Emma was so curt."

Gloria waved a hand. "But I understand! My niece told me all about Emma, and I'll admit, I'm green with envy. It must be wonderful to be a famous writer, and be so popular." She pointed at the newspaper on the table. "And she even has her picture in the paper!"

Wondering if Emma had been curt because she was stressed out over her "famous" writing career, or because

"Gorgeous Gloria" would be wearing *her* aprons and cleaning *her* house, Jennifer picked up the paper, and scanned the story. It was very flattering, and so was the picture. Finally, she said, "I'll be going to the market in a little while, Grandfather, so if you can help me make a list..."

Wes handed Jennifer a slip of paper. "Gloria already took inventory, and made up the list. I didn't hire her to do any cooking, but she says she's better at that than anything, and can cook up some special dishes for the freezer. I wasn't about to argue, because that chicken casserole we had last night cleaned us out, and the likelihood of Emma replenishing the freezer soon seems pretty remote."

Gloria made a face. "Well, I think I can do better than a chicken casserole."

Jennifer glanced at the list, and nearly swooned. Both sides of the paper were filled with the kinds of things you might find in California, but hardly in Calico, Nebraska. "I don't know if the market will have everything, Gloria. Like Monterey Bay sole? And shiitake mushrooms?"

The Pink Rabbit Caper

Gloria flushed. "Sorry. I keep forgetting where I am. The mushrooms are for Szechuan beef. Well, never mind. Just get what you can. I'm really very good at improvising."

Jennifer took the list, and hurried out of the house, suddenly in need of fresh air. She had the feeling Gorgeous Gloria was really *very* good at a lot of things, and worse, was seeing the curious light in her grandfather's eyes.

Jennifer took her time at the market and had no qualms about making substitutions, so by the time she had the cart piled high, she was convinced they weren't going to be forced to eat Szechuan beef, or frog's legs on a bed of curly endive. Unfortunately, she didn't fare as well with the continuous line of shoppers, who kept following her around, asking impossible questions. And one woman she'd never seen before even handed her a copy of the newspaper and said, "Tell Emma to be sure and autograph it right there, under the picture. And tell her I'll pick it up later this afternoon."

Jennifer looked at the smiling lady and said, "And you are?"

"Bonnie Brown. My husband and I are visiting the Babkinses. Maybe you know them?"

"I know them, but I'm sorry to say I can't help you, Mrs. Brown. If you want Emma's autograph, you'll have to talk to her."

Suddenly in need of fresh air again, Jennifer paid for her purchases, and quickly headed for the door. But before she could make her escape, she was confronted by Lolly Peabody, Penelope Davis, and Sabina Rider, who was a gymnastics teacher at the high school. At that point, she managed a smile, told them she had to get home before the carton of ice cream melted, and hurried out praying nobody followed her, and giving heartfelt thanks when nobody did.

In the parking lot, Jennifer quickly unloaded the bags from the shopping cart into the Jeep, and that was when she noticed the envelope addressed to Emma, wedged down in the bag of canned goods. Without a doubt, somebody had slipped a fan letter into her cart when she wasn't looking, and she had the feeling it was going to be the first of many.

Jennifer climbed into the Jeep, and sighed. For the first time in her life, she wasn't looking forward to going home.

Chapter Four

"This is for you," Jennifer said, tossing the envelope on her grandfather's desk in the study. "Somebody slipped it into the bag of canned goods while I was in the market."

Emma picked up the envelope and sighed. "Probably another citizen trying to tell me how I should write my story."

"Or maybe it's your first fan letter." Jennifer sat down in a cozy tube chair near the desk, and took comfort in the room she loved so much, with its dark wood paneling, rich leather furniture, and rows of books along the far wall. Emma had opened the window to the soft afternoon breeze, and sunlight filtered through the lacy curtains, creating a filigree pattern across the caramel-colored carpeting. The room had always been her sanctuary when she was a child—a place where she felt safe and loved—and it still affected her the same way.

"Grandfather made a pot of tea, if you'd like a cup," Jennifer said finally.

"Maybe later." Emma's eyes narrowed. "Is that woman still here?"

"She's in the kitchen with Grandfather. They're putting away the groceries, and then she's going to teach him how to make chicken piccata, whatever that is."

"Your granddaddy didn't hire that woman to do the cooking," Emma snapped.

"I know, but she offered, and Grandfather thought it was a good idea, because we don't have any meals left in the freezer, and . . ."

Emma's shoulders drooped. "And that's my fault. I'm sorry, honey. Guess I've gone a little overboard here, but I can't seem to get away from this story. I even think about it at night, when I should be sleeping. John, Jr., is going to print the first installment on Sunday, so maybe after that, I'll be able to relax."

"Are you worried about meeting your deadlines?"

"A little, I guess. . . . She seems nice enough."

"Gloria? She's okay. So, aren't you going to open your fan letter?"

Emma opened the envelope, pulled out a folded slip of paper, and sighed. "At first, I was flattered because so many nice things have been happening to me, but now I don't know, Jennifer. I think maybe it's gone too far. . . ." Emma frowned, read the note a second time, and uttered, "If that isn't the ticket!"

Jennifer read the typewritten note, and felt the hair at the nape of her neck rise.

Thought you should know, Emma. Your story is more truth than fiction. There really is a body buried some-

where in Calico, and I'm not talking about in the cemetery. Here is your first clue: Shadows from the courthouse plaza at four o'clock, will point the way to a whitewashed dock.

"Th-this has to be a prank," Jennifer said hesitantly. "Somebody's idea of a sick joke."

"Somebody's idea of a sick joke," Emma repeated, but her uneasy expression belied the words. "But I suppose we should show it to the sheriff, just the same."

"Show what to the sheriff?" Wes said, walking into the study with a handful of mail. "Charlie was late today. Mostly bills, and a letter for you, Emma. Postmarked here in Calico. Bet it's a fan letter."

"That's what I thought this was," Jennifer said, handing him the note.

Wes read the note, and shook his head. "This has to be a joke."

Emma had opened the second envelope, and said, "Or somebody is using my plot to make a confession. Listen to this:

Emma,
Red sky in the morning, sailor take warning. Five o'clock sharp, five minutes west, no time to rest. Just look to your right, and you'll see the light.

"Joke or contrived confession, now we definitely have to tell the sheriff," Wes said.

Jennifer said, "Sheriff Cody will want to see the notes, and with Gloria here..."

Emma rolled her eyes. "If our fine Calico residents find out about this... Well, I don't want to even *think* about the outcome."

Jennifer nodded. "You're busy with your story, Emma, and Grandfather is going to spend the afternoon learning to make chicken piccata, so I'll take the notes to the sheriff."

Emma made a face. "Chicken piccata. It sounds dreadful. What's in it?"

"I have no idea," Wes said with a grin. "But we're going to package it for the freezer."

Emma harrumphed. "Well, maybe I can get finished up early, so I can help you."

Jennifer left the house a few minutes later with a smile on her face, because it had just occurred to her that having Gorgeous Gloria around might be exactly what Emma needed to get her feet back on the ground.

The sheriff's office was tucked in beside City Hall, and a block from the courthouse. It was only three-thirty, so Jennifer had plenty of time to talk to the sheriff before going to the courthouse, where "shadows were supposed to point the way to a whitewashed dock at four o'clock." She couldn't believe that she was actually considering following the clues, and was still shaking her head when she walked into the sheriff's modest but efficient office.

Sheriff Cody looked up from the files on his desk, and smiled. "Well, this is a surprise, young lady. You just missed Nettie. She went home to work on her story. To hear her talk, she couldn't wait to get started. Says Emma is her inspiration. That writing class must be something. Sorry I missed all the fun last night."

Jennifer sat down in the chair beside the oversized desk, and handed him the notes. "It's *something*, all right. Has Nettie told you anything about Emma's plot?"

"Uh-huh, along with half the town. Everybody is talking about it, and about how John, Jr., is going to run the story in the paper." He looked at the notes and frowned. "Is this somebody's idea of a joke?"

"I don't know, Sheriff." Jennifer pointed at the first note. "That one was slipped into one of my grocery bags while I was in the market earlier today. The second note came in the mail this afternoon."

"Postmarked in Calico. Both notes were typed on the same typewriter. Take a look at the E in Emma's name. It's darker than the other letters, and a little crooked. If the note was put in your grocery bag, the person who did it had to be standing near the checkout stand."

Jennifer helped herself to a cup of coffee, and tried to recreate the scene. "Marie

Wessler was in line directly behind me, and that tall blond kid with the big ears was bagging, and Connie was the checker.''

"Did the bag boy help you out with your groceries?"

"No, I pushed the cart myself."

"Did you talk to anybody on the way to the parking lot?"

"I talked to Lolly Peabody, Penelope Davis, and Sabina Rider for a few minutes before I went out the door, but I didn't talk to anybody in the parking lot. I only had one thought on my mind at the time, and that was how much I was going to dread going home. I found the note in the bag when I was putting it into the Jeep. I thought it might be a fan letter."

"Some fan letter. So I'd say we have five suspects. Have to count out Marie Wessler, because she was behind you."

"But she was near my shopping cart when I was talking to Lolly, Penelope, and Sabina. She only had a few items to pay for, and stopped to say hello on her way out."

The sheriff opened a notebook. "You know the bag boy's name?"

"I think it's Terry. He's in high school, and works at the market part time."

"Parents?"

"His father works at the hospital. In Maintenance, I think."

"Okay. So, why were you dreading going home?"

"Grandfather hired Rose Kelly's aunt to help with the housework while Emma is finishing her story, and I can easily see the woman taking over. She's already taken over Emma's kitchen, and Emma is having a fit."

The sheriff scratched his chin. "Ah-ah, well if you're talking about Gloria Anderson, I can understand why Emma is upset. I saw Gloria in the coffee shop yesterday, and she wanted to know all about the eligible men in Calico, preferably men in good health, and over fifty years old."

Jennifer groaned. "That sounds like she's looking for a husband."

"Uh-huh, and she is one mighty fine-looking woman. I can think of quite a few eligible men who would be interested."

Jennifer frowned at the sheriff. "I hope you're not including Grandfather."

The sheriff shrugged. "And your grandfather is a mighty fine-looking man. That isn't a warning. Just an observation, and sometimes hearts can be led astray. It's called chemistry, Jennifer, and it isn't our place to reason why it happens; it just does.

"So, are you gonna follow these clues?"

"Will you think I'm crazy if I say yes?"

The sheriff gave her a lopsided grin. "No, because my curiosity has been aroused, too. Want some company? I was about to close up shop for the day anyway."

"I'd like that very much, Sheriff. Shall we walk?"

"And chance getting mobbed? I know it's only a block, but we want to make sure we're at the courthouse at four o'clock. We'll take my patrol car, park in the parking lot, and go from there."

Ten minutes later, they were standing in the courthouse plaza, studying the shadows as they inched across the grass. The time was 3:55.

At four straight up, they walked to the end of the longest shadow, created by a very tall tree, and the sheriff cleared his throat. "If we were to draw a straight line from here to the river, and followed it, we'd end up at Willow Landing."

Jennifer asked, "Is the dock whitewashed?"

"It is. Got a new coat a few weeks ago. Shall we give it a try? We can make it before five easily enough."

Jennifer nodded, and followed the sheriff to his car.

Willow Landing was a few miles east of White River Bridge, and was the closest place to town to launch a boat. And there were three docks. One running parallel with the river, and two jutting out on large pilings. Boats of all descriptions were moored on either side, and at the end of both, there was a spot for fishermen to try their hand from the dock. The boathouse was on the large dock, along with the bait and tackle shop.

The sheriff parked in the gravel lot beside the boathouse, and scratched his head. " 'Red sky in the morning, sailor take warning. Five minutes west, no time to rest. Just look to your right, and you'll see the light.' Does that mean five minutes west from the dock? And are we supposed to walk west along the riverbank?"

"I think we're supposed to take a boat, Sheriff Cody. That's why the note says 'sailor take warning.' And we definitely have to be five minutes west at five o'clock."

The sheriff puffed out his cheeks. "Well, I'd better tell you right now, I get seasick in the bathtub, and what I know about boats, you could put in the eye of a needle."

Jennifer smiled. "I know how to navigate a small motorboat. And I'm sure old Archie has one we can rent."

The sheriff gritted his teeth. "Guess I don't have a choice, huh?"

"Sure you do, Sheriff. You can stay here while I check it out."

"No way! I want to be there when you 'see the light.' "

"Then let's get the boat. The last place I want to be after dark is on the water."

"We've got a good two and a half hours left before it gets dark, Jennifer, and the note says we only have to go five minutes west."

"Uh-huh, but we don't know what else we'll find. Maybe we'll get lucky, and find another clue."

Old Archie Thorp had owned the boathouse for years, and was blind in one eye, and couldn't see out of the other. He was hard of hearing, too, and Jennifer had to shout at him to get him to understand what they wanted.

"You want a motorboat?" the old man said finally. "Kinda late to go fishin'. Most of the fishermen are already in. Kinda early in the season, too. Fish ain't biting."

Jennifer explained that they weren't going to fish, wouldn't be gone long, and gave him a twenty-dollar bill.

It was at that point old Archie realized Jennifer was with the sheriff, and gave them a yellow-toothed grin. "Police business, huh? Well, you just keep your money. You can take that white boat tied up over there." He waved a hand. "Or maybe it's tied up over there. Yeah, that's where it's gotta be. The dock to your left. Ya can't miss it. It's got a red outboard motor."

"Gas?"

"It's all gassed up and ready to go."

Jennifer thanked the man, and grinned up at the sheriff. "Ready?"

The sheriff grumbled, "No, but I'm not about to be outdone by a little lady who has more spunk than brains. Just don't tell Ida. We were down on the Republican River with her sister's family last year, and she claims I spoiled the whole day because I wouldn't go out on their new boat. And that one was a hardy cruiser."

In the boat finally, and with the motor running, Jennifer backed out of the slip and headed west. Within five minutes, they'd reached the spot on the river that was not only narrow, but full of rocks and rapids.

Boats were supposed to stay out of the area, and it was easy to see why.

"Now what?" the sheriff asked through clenched teeth. "Because we sure can't go any further."

"We could portage around, but I don't think that's what our friend had in mind. Look to your right, Sheriff."

The sheriff squinted through the late-afternoon sunlight, and grunted, "Whoa. Would you look at that!"

On the other side of the river, the water filtration plant rose to impressive heights, and near the top, sunlight reflected off the windows as brightly as a beacon at midnight. A few minutes later, the light was gone, as the sun lowered in the late-afternoon sky.

"I know I'm beginning to sound like a broken record," the sheriff muttered. "But now what?"

"Our answer is at the filtration plant," Jennifer told him. "Are you familiar with the layout?"

"I am. Ida's brother, Frank, is the night foreman."

"So, what's on the top floor?"

"The office, a meeting room, and a storage room."

Jennifer headed back to Willow Landing. "I'd say we'd better check out all three rooms, Sheriff, but we'll have to take your car, because there is no place to dock the boat near the plant."

The sheriff finally managed a smile. "Gotta tell you, young lady. That's the best news I've had all day."

It was after six when they made their way up the outside steps to the top floor of the water filtration plant, and this time, it was Jennifer who was complaining about the height. The sheriff reciprocated by saying, "You can always stay on the ground while I check it out."

Jennifer's response was immediate. "No way! If you could survive the boat, I can survive this!"

"So, we both have our crosses to bear," the sheriff said, opening the door to the office.

A pretty blond woman sat at a desk inside the musty-smelling room, and when she saw the sheriff, a smile lit up her face. "Sheriff Cody! You just missed Frank. He had to go downstairs."

The sheriff raised a hand. "That's okay, June. We're here on official business. Well, kind of. This is June Davis, Jennifer, and June, this is Jennifer Gray, the pastor's granddaughter. We're looking for an envelope. Might be addressed to Emma Morrison."

The woman's brows drew together in a frown. "And it's supposed to be here?"

"We're not sure," Jennifer said. "Is this the room that gets the late-afternoon sunlight?"

"No, that would be the storage room. We used to have our office in there, but couldn't handle it. Too bright. We tried putting up shades, but then the room would get stifling."

"Have you seen anybody around today who doesn't belong here?" Jennifer asked.

"No, I surely haven't," the woman said.

The sheriff spoke up. "Can we take a look in the storage room?"

June Davis nodded. "It's down the hall, second door on your right. I'd go with you, but I have to finish the payroll, and I'm already on overtime."

As they made their way down the hall, Jennifer could hear the hum of heavy equipment far below, and she couldn't help but wonder, *if* there was another clue on the premises, how it had ended up here.

The sheriff must have been thinking the same thing, because a few minutes later, he said, "You know, it just occurred to me that our note writer has given this whole thing a lot of thought."

"I know," Jennifer replied. "I'd say about as much thought as Emma has given her story. It's like some sort of a creeping virus has taken over their lives."

The sheriff grinned. "Too bad Emma isn't writing a science fiction story, and then she could write about a 'creeping virus' that has taken over her life. Ida has a movie video about something like that. I think it's called *The Pod People*."

"That's gross," Jennifer said with a shudder. "This is the door..."

The sheriff nodded, and opened the door.

The room was filled with crates and boxes, and Jennifer sighed. "I wouldn't know where to begin to look."

"If it's here, it's gotta be out in plain sight, Jennifer. You take one side, and I'll take the other."

Five minutes later, the sheriff found the note wedged in between two boxes, but with enough of it showing to be easily spotted, and exclaimed, "Bingo!"

"You open it, Sheriff."

The sheriff opened it, and read:

Emma, you're one smart lady to get this far, but then we all know how smart you are, because you are writing that wonderful story about that wonderful detective searching through all those compelling clues. I expect by now, you've already brought the sheriff into this. I have no problem with that. Two heads are always better than one. And now, I will give you the next two clues:

1. The cemetery at midnight is a

spooky sight. Especially on a moon-bright night. Try for the little rise near the back service gate, and let the moonbeams decide your fate.

2. Let your nose lead the way, to a bright new day. Chocolate frosting and sprinkles will add calories, not wrinkles. One for the money, two for the show, three to get ready, and four to go.

Jennifer took the note, and sat down on a box. "The cemetery at midnight? Wonderful."

"It sounds like you have to be there at midnight to get the benefit of the moonlight. Sort of like the sunlight up here. But what's with the chocolate frosting and sprinkles?"

Jennifer sighed. "Let your nose lead the way to a bright new day. It has to be the doughnut shop, Sheriff Cody. When they are baking doughnuts early each morning, the mouth-watering aroma wafts all through the whole town. Unfortunately, we won't be able to 'follow our noses' until tomorrow morning."

The sheriff patted his belly. "I put on five pounds if I get within two blocks of the doughnut shop. So, I take it you're going out to the cemetery tonight?"

"Yes, but I won't be alone. I'll take Grandfather with me, and if you'd like to come along..."

"If you don't mind, I think I'll sit this one out," the sheriff said quickly. "You can give me a report when we go to the doughnut shop in the morning. And don't be misled if I sound a little indifferent, Jennifer, because that isn't what it is. I just have a *thing* against cemeteries, especially at night, and Ida would have a fit if she knew what I was up to. It's bad enough when I get a legitimate call in the middle of the night. Not that this isn't a legitimate dilemma, but, well, you know what I mean."

Jennifer knew exactly what he meant, and gave him a compassionate smile. "Then I'll meet you at the doughnut shop at seven in the morning?"

The Pink Rabbit Caper

"At seven. And be careful tonight, Jennifer. We don't know what kind of a person we're dealing with here, and until we put some of the puzzle pieces together..."

"I know. I'll watch my back, and carry a big stick."

When they went through the office to get to the outside stairs, June Davis was so engrossed in the mound of work on her desk, she didn't even look up.

"Wonder if she'd hear the fire alarm if it went off," the sheriff said, as they started down the stairs.

"Probably not, and that might be how the note writer got by her so easily. I mean, if she was distracted..."

"Or maybe he didn't have to get by her. Maybe he knows her. You asked her if she'd seen anybody around who didn't belong here. What if he's an employee? Or a delivery person?"

"He could have come in through the plant, too," Jennifer returned. "Maybe you'd better talk to June again."

The sheriff looked at his watch. "I will, and I plan on talking to my brother-in-law, too, but it will have to be tomorrow. I promised Ida I'd be home early, and I still have to take you back to the office so you can get your Jeep. Meanwhile, remember what I said. Be careful. I think the guy has every detail planned, right down the line, only he thinks it's Emma who is following the clues. He might not appreciate having you as a substitution."

They'd reached the patrol car before Jennifer asked, "Do you think he could be dangerous?"

"I don't know, Jennifer, but if there really is a body, and he's the killer, it's hard to second-guess how he wants this to end."

It was also hard to think of the note writer as a man, because all along, Jennifer had had the impression they were dealing with a woman.

It was after seven when Jennifer walked into the cluttered, smelly kitchen, and found Emma and Wes in the middle of a heated debate.

Wes gave Jennifer a sheepish shrug, and muttered, "Gloria was going to clean things up, but Emma ordered her out of the house."

Emma's response was immediate. "I couldn't stand having that woman in my kitchen one minute longer!" She waved a hand as she harrumphed. "Will you just look at this mess, Jennifer? And if *this* isn't bad enough, she had the nerve to suggest working in *my* garden! And even worse than that, the chicken piccata turned out so dreadful, I had to toss it in the garbage."

"It wasn't *that* bad," Wes said glumly.

Emma raised her chin. "It was disgusting, and you know it, Wesley Gray. So now I have to come up with something else to fix for supper, and hope it will mask the stench."

"Cabbage and fish might do it," Jennifer said, trying to hold back the grin. Just having Emma in the kitchen again, for whatever reason, was wonderful.

Emma dipped a sponge in the sinkful of soapy water, and tackled the splatters on the wall above the stove. "Well, we don't have any fish, and what am I going to fix with cabbage at this late hour?"

"I told Emma if she couldn't stand the smell, open the windows," Wes said, "and she said she didn't want to offend the neighbors. I tried to remind her we don't have a neighbor within 'smelling' distance, but she was beyond reason."

Jennifer rummaged around in the spice cupboard, and came up with a handful of whole cloves, cinnamon sticks, and allspice. "Let's try simmering this in a little water, Emma. It's what you always do over the holidays when you want the house to smell festive. And as far as supper is concerned, why don't we just have tuna sandwiches and tomato soup?"

Emma's mouth turned down. "Your granddaddy was all set to have that fancy chicken dish, Jennifer, so I think I can do better than that."

Wanting to remind Emma that for the last week she hadn't cared what they ate, but knowing when to leave well enough alone, Jennifer suggested, "Then let's cook up some fettucini, and toss in a can of clams and fresh veggies."

Emma pursed her lips. "Well, I suppose

that would be okay." Big sigh. "I've made a decision, Jennifer. I'm going to keep working on my story, but only for a few hours each day. That way, I'll have plenty of time to take care of the house and do the cooking."

"Does that mean Gloria won't be coming back?" Jennifer asked, putting the spices in a pan.

Emma took the pan, added water, and placed it on the stove. "That's exactly what it means. I told you this afternoon I thought my writing was getting out of hand, and having that woman in the house today simply proved it. This house is my responsibility, and my home, and that's the way it stands."

"She needs the job," Wes tried to reason.

Emma harrumphed. "She doesn't need a job, she wants a husband, and you were just too blind to see it."

"Oh, I don't know about that, but I'll have to admit I was kinda flattered by all that attention," Wes said, with a twinkle in his eye.

"Attention?" Emma scoffed. "Why, I've never seen so much eyelash flapping and flirting in my life!" Her eyes narrowed over Jennifer. "You've been gone a good long time, young lady, and I know that 'look.' You took those notes to the sheriff, and . . . ?"

"Maybe we should discuss it after supper, Emma."

"And maybe we should discuss it right now. Here we are, arguing about that woman who doesn't count for one hill of beans, while you have something important to tell us."

Jennifer pulled the latest note out of her purse, and handed it to her grandfather. "The sheriff and I followed the clues, and ended up in a storage room at the water filtration plant, and that's where we found this. The 'light' was the sun reflecting off the windows, and we think the moonlight at the cemetery at midnight will point the way again."

Emma gasped. "The cemetery at midnight?"

Wes read the note, and shook his head.

"You'd better read this, Emma, before Jennifer tells us how they got from point A to B, and ended up at the filtration plant."

Emma wiped her hands and read the note. "It's full of compliments on the one hand, and full of scary stuff, too. You can't possibly be thinking about going out to the cemetery at midnight, Jennifer."

"I'll go, if Grandfather will go with me."

Emma grumbled, "And why can't the sheriff handle it?"

Not wanting Emma to know how the sheriff felt about the cemetery, Jennifer said, "He's busy tonight. But I am meeting him tomorrow morning at the bakery."

Wes said, "You think the second part of the clue refers to the bakery?"

" 'Let your nose lead the way,' and the mention of chocolate frosting and sprinkles suggests that, Grandfather."

Emma had put on a clean apron, and had water on for the pasta, before she said, "How on earth did you pinpoint the filtration plant?"

Jennifer told them while she set the table, finally adding, "So it's possible the note writer is familiar with the filtration plant, so that suggests it's a man. It's funny, because all along, I thought we were dealing with a woman."

"Maybe he's an employee," Wes said thoughtfully.

"Isn't Ida's brother the foreman?" Emma asked.

"Night foreman. The sheriff is going to question him tomorrow, along with June Davis. It's possible she saw something, but isn't aware of it. He's playing a game, just like the note writer in your story is playing a game with Jake Lamont, Emma, and I think we're going to have to play along, if we hope to find the answers."

Wes said, "So we're going out to the cemetery at midnight. Boy, oh boy. This guy has some imagination."

Emma grumbled, "Well, there is no way I'd make Jake Lamont go poking around the cemetery at midnight. Gives me a case of the shivers just thinking about it."

It gave Jennifer the shivers thinking about it, too, but she shrugged it off, and managed a smile. "Look on the bright side, Emma. The note writer truly appreciates your writing, otherwise he wouldn't be going to all this trouble to confess."

Emma frowned. "Do you really think that's what he's doing?"

"Yes, I do. And when he's ready to turn himself in, we'll get the last clue."

Wes's blue eyes darkened in thought. "Which brings to mind something that hasn't been addressed, sweetheart. What does he want to confess to? Writing the notes? Or the fact he killed someone, and buried the body?"

"There is one other possibility," Jennifer reasoned. "He isn't the killer, but simply knows the crime was committed, and knows where the body is buried."

"My note writer is the killer," Emma announced. "Only she thinks she's smarter than Jake. She figures Jake won't come close to finding the bodies for ages and ages, and expects him to run around in circles, and go a little crazy while he's doing it."

Wes gave Emma an exasperated glance.

"I thought this was supposed to be a short story, Emma. I mean, if Jake isn't supposed to find the bodies for 'ages' . . ."

Emma shrugged. "It is supposed to be a story, but the way the pages are piling up, it might end up book-length after all. Of course, if I slow down some, it'll take a lot longer to write, but I don't think John, Jr., will mind. He doesn't have to print an installment *every* week."

Wes sighed. "Well, let's hope our note writer doesn't expect us to run around in circles, trying to find the body. *If* there actually is a body. Did you ask the sheriff if he's had any missing person reports, sweetheart?"

"No, but wouldn't you think if somebody actually was missing in Calico, he would have said something about it?"

"You would think. How are you going to handle that in your story, Emma? Your lady killed five husbands, and buried their bodies in her rose garden. How does she explain their disappearance to the folks in White River?"

Emma frowned in thought. "To tell you

the truth, I don't know. I haven't thought that far ahead."

"Did all the husbands live in White River?" Jennifer asked.

Emma's frown deepened. "I haven't figured that out yet, either."

Wes said, "Uh-huh. So why don't we put our heads together, and try to give Emma a helping hand, sweetheart? In doing so, it might even help us solve our own little mystery. Unless, of course, Emma doesn't want our help."

Emma gave Wes a wan smile. "Are you thinking about all those suggestions the citizens of Calico gave me, that I had you throw out?"

"I can appreciate your independence, Emma, but yeah, I guess you could say that. I wouldn't want you to think we're interfering."

Emma gave Wes a hug. "If you two have any suggestions, I would be happy to hear them."

Delighted to have something to think about other than the cemetery at midnight, Jennifer eagerly joined in while they discussed Emma's plot. And she was amazed at the wonderful light she could see in her grandfather's eyes. And this time the light was directed at Emma, and Jennifer suddenly knew why. He was a part of Emma's writing now, and that was all he'd ever wanted. Simply to be able to share her hopes and dreams, as well as her problems, and not be left out. That's how it was—how it was supposed to be—after a lifelong friendship full of caring and love, and it wasn't only beautiful, it was wonderful.

Chapter Five

"I wonder what would have happened if this was a cloudy night?" Wes said, maneuvering his sedan along the bumpy road.

"I don't think our note writer has set a time limit on any of this," Jennifer replied, looking out at the familiar scenery that was now bathed in moonlight. The cemetery was two miles west of town, and a good mile off River Road. And although the cemetery was well maintained by Bert Levy, the caretaker, the road leading into it was not, because the property belonged to the town, and there never seemed to be enough money in the coffer to make the repairs. Before Willy was elected mayor, he had promised to get the necessary funding to repair all the problem spots around town, and still have a balanced budget, but he hadn't counted on the archaic town fathers to oppose him. Nor had he realized just how sparse the town treasury was. And so, for the moment, his hands were tied, though he had suggested at the last town meeting that the families who had loved ones buried in the cemetery might consider donating the money to make the repairs. He had backed that up by telling the disgruntled crowd that unless something was done soon, nobody was going to be able to get into the cemetery without a four-wheel-drive vehicle.

At that moment, Wes hit a bump, and if it hadn't been for the seat belt, Jennifer would have hit her head on the roof.

Wes pulled in under a stand of trees, and muttered, "That does it. I sure don't need a flat tire or a broken axle. We're almost there, so let's walk the rest of the way."

Jennifer sighed. "I was out here just a

month ago, and it didn't seem this bad. Now I'm sorry we didn't bring the Jeep.''

"It looks different in the daylight, sweetheart, because you can see all the ruts and potholes before you reach them.''

Glad she'd brought a jacket, because there was still a nip in the air, Jennifer trudged along beside her grandfather, and wondered if their midnight excursion was a mistake. Because the cemetery looked different at night, too, and eerie was the only way to describe it. Usually, she enjoyed coming here, because it was where her parents, grandmother, and great-grandparents were buried, and it was such a beautiful spot, full of flowers and trees. Yet now, even though Wes had brought along a flashlight to illuminate their way, the trees resembled black, ghostly creatures, and tiny night critters were skittering among the shrubbery and flowers. Only the headstones were clearly outlined in the moonlight, but for those in the shadows of the trees.

Wes took Jennifer's hand, and squeezed. "I know, you don't have to say it. Maybe this was a mistake. The nearest house is at least a mile away, so if... Never mind. I'm just being foolish."

"You're being cautious," Jennifer replied. "And I know what you were going to say. If the note writer is dangerous, this would be a good place for an ambush. We could scream our heads off, and nobody would hear us."

"Well, I wasn't going to put it that way, exactly, but you're close."

"What time is it?" Jennifer asked.

Wes put the beam of light on his wristwatch. "Eleven fifty-five. Five minutes to get to the service gate. Let's take the pathway to our left. It's the shortest route."

Just then, something skittered across Jennifer's sneakers, and she stifled a scream.

"It was only a lizard, or something that looked like a lizard," Wes grumbled. But he held Jennifer's hand a little tighter.

Trying to take comfort in the softness of the breeze, and the rich aroma of freshly turned earth, and her grandfather's warm hand, Jennifer peered through the shadows, trying to see the service gate ahead of them. Once there, they were supposed to find a little rise, and let the moonlight show them the way. Was it possible they would end up searching every inch of the cemetery before the night was over?

"There we are," Wes said. "Straight ahead. And there's the rise. Guess we should've brought along the clue, because I don't remember the exact wording. Are we supposed to stand on the rise?"

"It didn't really say, Grandfather. Just said we should *try* for the little rise near the back service gate, and let the moonbeams decide our fate."

"Fate. Now that's an interesting word. It could mean luck, but it could also mean doom."

Jennifer shivered, and looked at the monstrous earth-moving equipment parked by the back gate. *Giant night creatures,* she thought, pulling her jacket around her.

They were standing just below the rise now, and Wes cleared his throat. "We might as well climb up to the top. You with me?"

Jennifer nodded, but what she really wanted to do was turn around and run.

When they reached the top, they were bathed in moonlight, but there were no revelation like there had been on the river, with the sun reflecting off the windows of the filtration plant. Wes turned off the flashlight and grumbled, "This one might be a wild-goose chase."

Jennifer was beginning to think it had been a wasted trip, when she saw the flash of white. It was on the other side of the rise, near the fence.

Wes saw it, too, and said, "Boy, oh boy. That has to be the envelope. Wait here, and I'll get it."

Even though Wes wasn't going to be more than ten feet away, Jennifer shook her head vigorously, and stammered, "I-I'll go with you. . . ."

The ten feet were more like twenty, and the grass was higher here, and wet. Jennifer's canvas shoes were soaked by the time they reached the envelope. It was obvious the automatic sprinklers had been on, but the game player had thought of everything, because the envelope was encased in plastic.

"I'd suggest we take this back to the car and read it," Wes said, removing the envelope from the plastic covering. "But my gut feeling tells me we're not through in the cemetery." He used the flashlight to read the note, and Jennifer held her breath.

You are on your own, Emma. Sorry for the dilemma. Latona B. Marshell, beloved mother and wife. Somewhere in the cemetery, still laughing at life.

"Uh-huh," Wes said. "Well, I think I've got the picture. We're supposed to find Latona B. Marshell's headstone."

"So who is Latona B. Marshell?"

"Part of Calico's history, I would say. Some of the dates on the headstones go back a long way, sweetheart. Back to covered wagon days. How about if we save this for tomorrow, when we can look for it in the sunlight. We have the name. That's enough for now."

Jennifer made a sweeping motion with

her hand. "Wasn't the original cemetery over there, by that stand of peachleaf willows?"

Wes grinned. "It sure was. You want to take a look before we call it a night?"

"We've come this far, Grandfather, and we have a flashlight.... Why come back tomorrow if we don't have to?"

Wes's answer was a grunt, as he led the way down the rise.

Five minutes later, they were standing in front of Latona B. Marshell's headstone (1845–1885), staring at the bouquet of red creeper roses, and at the note—also encased in plastic—attached to the red ribbon.

Wes handed Jennifer the bouquet, and read the note.

Roses are red, violets are blue. Sleep well tonight, Emma, and tomorrow, we will begin anew.

Wes tucked the note in a pocket, and gave Jennifer a hug. "What do you say we go home and worry about tomorrow, tomorrow?''

Jennifer nodded, but it wasn't until they'd reached the car that she realized she was still carrying the bouquet. But what was even stranger, was knowing there was no way she could leave it behind.

Emma was still up when they got home, and her greeting wasn't a surprise. "This has been the worst two hours of my life! I've been so worried." And then she looked at the roses, and frowned. "I hope you're not going to tell me you swiped that bouquet off some poor departed soul's grave!"

"The flowers were for us," Wes said, "along with two notes. One by the back service gate, and the other one attached to the bouquet. And to tell you the truth, none of it makes any sense. I've been thinking about it all the way home. Each clue leads to another clue, but to what end? We could spend the next year running around town getting nowhere."

Emma said, "Well, I'm sure that's exactly what the dolt has in mind. I was thinking just tonight that I might have Jake stop traipsing all over after the clues, just to see how the killer reacts. Of course, he doesn't know the note writer is the killer, yet. Maybe that's what we should do, and see what happens." Her eyes narrowed. "I surely hope you don't plan on keeping that bouquet in the house, Jennifer. Just knowing that crazy person touched it gives me the creeps."

Jennifer dumped the roses in the trash, and sighed. "I don't even know why I brought it home, Emma. And that gives *me* the creeps. The whole thing was creepy. Does the name Latona B. Marshell mean anything to you?"

Emma's brows drew together. "Seems to me I've heard that name somewhere. Why?"

"Because the roses and the second note were on her grave. She was born in 1845, and died in 1885."

"And was obviously the wife of one of Calico's founders. I'll call Penelope Davis in the morning. She knows more about the town's history than I do. You look frozen clear through, Jennifer. I have the water on for tea.''

"I think I'd just rather go to bed, Emma. It's been a long day, and I have to get up early in the morning."

Wes said, "Because you have to meet the sheriff at the doughnut shop at seven. Can't imagine what kind of a clue will come out of that."

"Well, if it turns out to be an important one, I'll call you."

Emma wagged a finger. "And don't forget, we have class tomorrow night. Hopefully, now that John, Jr., is going to print my story in the paper, we won't have the mob we had last night. Wait, was that only last night? It seems like a year ago."

Jennifer gave hugs around, and went upstairs, but her thoughts were on the red creeper roses. And once again, she felt a tug of apprehension, and that elusive feeling that the answers were so close, she could almost reach out and touch them. Were they running around in circles? Or did each clue actually mean something significant, and they were simply missing it?

Before she went to bed, Jennifer listed all the clues on a sheet of paper, skipping over the "chatty" words addressed to Emma.

The shadows in the courthouse plaza, that led them to the dock, and then, to the filtration plant, where they found the second and third clues. The first note in the cemetery, that led them to the red roses on Latona B. Marshell's grave.

Jennifer wrote down: *Filtration plant, red creeper roses, and Latona B. Marshell,* underlined all three, and went to bed.

Chapter Six

At five to seven the next morning, Jennifer walked into the doughnut shop and found the sheriff and Ken Hering sitting at a corner table, eating doughnuts and drinking coffee. She joined them, stifled a yawn, but managed an appreciative smile, because the sheriff had already ordered her a cup of coffee.

"Okay," the sheriff said after she was seated. "We're here, so here we go again. Now what?"

Jennifer shrugged. "I haven't the foggiest idea, Sheriff Cody. Did you tell Ken what happened yesterday?"

"I did, and I told him what you were going to do last night."

Ken shook his head. "Tell me you didn't go out to the cemetery at midnight."

"I did, and Grandfather went with me." She showed them the notes, told them about the grave and red creeper roses, and waited.

"It's a game that could have you running all over town forever," Ken said finally.

"That's what Grandfather is afraid of, and to what end? He's beginning to think it's nothing more than a game, and it's being played at our expense. I probably didn't sleep much more than two hours last night, and I feel like a rag. And I know Emma didn't sleep well, either, because I heard her in the exercise room before daybreak."

At that moment, Betty, the waitress, walked up to the table and handed Jennifer a bag. "Hi, Jennifer. This is Emma's order. Four chocolate doughnuts. Is she coming in this morning?"

"No, and Emma didn't order... Ummm, well, thanks, but she didn't place the order personally. Do you remember who did?"

The waitress scrunched her brows. "Gee, I don't know. The order came in by phone early yesterday, and the person said Emma would be in sometime this morning."

"Male or female?"

"Gee, again I don't know. We were really busy, so I didn't pay much attention. If you think she'd rather have glazed or plain cake..."

"No, this is fine. How much do I owe you?"

"The order has already been paid for. Found an envelope under the door when I came in this morning. A note and two dollars. The note said the money was to pay for Emma's doughnut order, and I'll admit I thought it was strange." She grinned. "But then the whole world seems to be full of strange people these days."

"Do you still have the note?" the sheriff asked.

"I'll look, though it probably got tossed out with the trash."

When the waitress hurried off to wait on a customer, Jennifer handed the bag to the sheriff, and took a deep breath. "*You* look inside."

The sheriff opened the bag, and shook his head. "No envelope, no note. Just four chocolate doughnuts."

"Now I'm really confused," Jennifer said.

"The clue had to be on that note that got tossed out with the trash," Ken reasoned.

"Emma said she's going to stop her detective from running around, chasing down clues, just to see how the killer will react, and suggested we do the same thing. Now it looks like we'll be forced to, because the chain has been broken, and there is no way we can let our note writer know we didn't get the next clue."

Ken said, "Short of taking an ad out in the paper." He made a frame with his hands. "I can see it now. 'Attention, you out there, who is sending Emma Morrison all the notes and clues. Missed the last clue because it went out with the trash. Please send duplicate.' Sorry, Jennifer, but the whole thing is so outrageous, it's hard to take it seriously.''

Jennifer nodded. ''I know, and that's exactly what's keeping us on the trail.''

A few minutes later, the waitress was back, and handed Jennifer a slip of paper. ''Here it is. The boss put it in the register. You know, underneath the tray, where we keep the checks.''

With her heart up in her throat, Jennifer read the note, but found it to be just what the waitress said it was. *I've enclosed two dollars to pay for Emma Morrison's doughnuts,* it said. *Thanks.*

''No clues there,'' Jennifer said, tossing the note on the table. ''Other than the fact it was typed on the same typewriter. Look at the E in 'Emma.' ''

''Bummer,'' Ken said.

''Unless . . .''

The sheriff's eyes were bright. ''Unless . . . ?''

''The bag of doughnuts is the clue. Do

you remember what the clue said, Sheriff?''

"Ah, something about letting your nose lead the way, and wrinkles."

"Oh, brother." Ken chuckled.

" 'Let your nose lead the way, to a bright new day. Chocolate frosting and sprinkles will add calories, not wrinkles. One for the money, two for the show, three to get ready, and four to go.' Maybe that translates into four chocolate doughnuts to go."

Ken shook his head. "You've gotta wonder about this guy. He must stay up all night thinking up this stuff."

Jennifer sighed. "And he's no doubt enjoying every minute of it. I'll take the doughnuts to the clinic. Maybe if I keep looking at them long enough, I'll get a brainstorm."

"Are you guys going to class tonight?" Ken asked.

"It depends on how I feel later on. I know Emma is planning to go."

"I'd like to sit in again, if she wouldn't mind."

"Emma? Can't imagine why she would, but I'm curious, Ken. Are you expecting another mob?"

"No, but I'd like to observe the students. It just occurred to me that this guy is probably in your class."

"Emma's plot hasn't been restricted to the class," Jennifer told him. "Almost everybody in town knew what she was doing, and about the plot, after that night she read the beginning of her story."

"Yeah, but I'd say the most creative minds are probably in that class."

"Well, if it's a man, it has to be Orris Ford, the butcher. Now, you tell me. Does he look that creative to you?"

Ken smiled. "Can't always tell a book by its cover, though I'm not counting out the fact that it might be a woman, either. I'd also like to get a look at their papers, and check for that misaligned E."

The sheriff nodded. "That's a good idea, and it would sure point the finger in the right direction. I plan on talking to June and Frank over at the filtration plant later today. If I find out anything, I'll call you at the clinic, Jennifer.''

Feeling more and more dejected by the minute, and slightly nauseated from the rich aroma of the chocolate doughnuts, Jennifer walked out into the sun-splashed morning and headed for the clinic, convinced they were all a little mad to be playing this silly game.

Jennifer was taking a lunch break out in the garden area behind the clinic when Ben joined her, carrying an envelope. "This came in the mail, Jennifer, and it's addressed to you. Take a look at the E."

Jennifer looked at the bold, slightly crooked letter, and sighed. "You open it, Ben."

Ben opened the envelope, and read:

Jennifer. It took me a while to figure it out, but now that I have, I thought a personal note might be in order. At first, I was disappointed to hear you've been following my clues instead of Emma, but now that I've had time to think about it, I understand. She is a very busy lady, and it was presumptuous of me to assume she was going to drop everything because I expected her to.

And so, I forgive her, and you.

You might be thinking this is all a joke right about now, and I can understand that, too. But it isn't. I swear to you on my great-grandmother's grave, it isn't. And not only that, each and every clue is valid. All you have to do is put them together, and you'll have your answers.

Are you ready for your next clue? Clear your mind now, Jennifer, and concentrate.

A long stretch of road, a tree on a hill. A row of corn, and doctor bills.

That's it until next time.

Jennifer groaned. "And I'm supposed to make something out of that? It's as bad as the doughnuts."

Ben gave Jennifer's hand a pat. "Go home, kiddo. Tina will be here in about an hour, and you look exhausted. Take tomorrow off, too. Irene will be here to do the books, so I won't be alone. If we have an emergency, I'll call you."

"To use one of Ken's favorite expressions, this really is a bummer, Ben. I'm running around in circles, feeling like a fool, and I'm neglecting everything that's important to me."

"If that's your way of saying you're a little distracted, hey, you don't have to apologize. As I see it, you have one whopping mystery to solve, and nobody is going to get any rest until you do. So have at it, Jennifer. Give it everything you've got, and I'll put my money on you."

Jennifer got up and gave Ben a hug. "You're the best, Ben Copeland, and I mean that from the bottom of my heart."

Wes was out in the garden, absently pulling up weeds, when Jennifer made her way along the flagstone pathway between the church and the house. And she knew something was wrong the minute she saw his face.

The Pink Rabbit Caper

He stood up, wiped the perspiration from his brow with a handkerchief, and muttered, "I hope your morning was better than mine. Emma has writer's block, and she's in a snit. Go talk to her, sweetheart. Maybe you can reason with her, and convince her it isn't the end of the world. And while you're at it, tell her I've already made a big fruit salad, and I'm barbecuing hot dogs for lunch. Maybe that will put a smile on her face."

Now didn't seem like the appropriate time to tell him about the doughnuts, or the letter, so Jennifer simply kissed his cheek, and went into the unusually quiet house. No radio, no TV, no music, no Emma puttering around in the kitchen.

Jennifer finally found her in her bedroom, stretched out on the white chenille bedspread with a cold washcloth over her eyes and forehead. Concerned, Jennifer sat down on the edge of the bed, and asked, "Are you ill, Emma?"

Emma removed the washcloth, and pinched her eyes shut with her fingers. "I have writer's block, and I thought if I lay here nice and quiet, it might help. But it hasn't, and now I have a headache. I've already called Judith, to tell her I won't be going to class tonight.''

"But surely you have enough written to read."

"I wouldn't be reading anyway, Jennifer. When it was decided that John, Jr., would print my story, I agreed not to read any more of it in class."

"So what's the problem?"

"I can't face those folks, knowing I have writer's block. It would be a drag on the whole class."

"It will be a drag if you don't show up," Jennifer reasoned. "They are counting on you for inspiration."

"And that's exactly why I can't go." Emma opened one eye. "You're home early. Slow day at the clinic?"

"No, not really. Ben just thought I needed some time off to work on our mystery. I'm off tomorrow, too, unless we have an emergency. Did you call Penelope Davis?"

The Pink Rabbit Caper

"I did, but she's in North Platte for the day."

Jennifer pulled the envelope out of her purse. "This came in the mail today, addressed to me at the clinic."

Emma read the letter, and sat up. "What about the doughnut shop? Did you find a clue there?"

"Just four chocolate doughnuts," Jennifer said, and went on to explain.

Emma harrumphed. "Well, my clues in my story were better. At least they meant something. They might have had Jake Lamont running around in circles, but at least they were leading him in the right direction."

"And who's to say these clues aren't? You read the letter, Emma. The person said the clues are valid, and all we have to do is put them all together to get the answers."

Emma studied the letter. "A long stretch of road, a tree on a hill, a row of corn... I know I've seen that somewhere before, Jennifer." She sniffed. "Do I smell the barbecue?"

"You do. Grandfather is barbecuing hot dogs, and he's already made the fruit salad. He wants to put a smile on your face."

"And what does he say about the new clues and the letter?"

"I haven't told him yet...."

Emma held up a hand. "Somebody is talking to your granddaddy. A female voice. If that's Gloria Anderson..."

Emma's bedroom overlooked the patio area where Wes had set up the barbecue, and Jennifer peeked out the window. "Wonderful. It's Lolly Peabody. Just the person to have around when you have a headache."

Emma stood up, and brushed down her tan-colored slacks. "Well, I can take Lolly a lot better than I can take Gloria. Do you know, that woman had the nerve to call your granddaddy this morning, and invite him on a picnic? Her treat. You go on out now, and let me freshen up."

"Emma will be out in a few minutes," Jennifer said when she joined Wes and Lolly on the patio.

Looking garish but attractive in a white

beaded dress, red spiky shoes, and a red, feathery headband, Lolly gave Jennifer a fetching smile. "Hello, Jennifer. When I heard Emma wasn't coming to class tonight, and why, I just had to come over. Came so fast, I plum forgot Homer."

Taken aback for a moment, because "Homer" was Lolly's late husband, and then realizing Lolly was talking about the pink rabbit, Jennifer returned her smile. "I didn't know you named the rabbit Homer."

"Well, it's fitting, don't you think? I mean, Homer gave me that bunny the Easter before he..." She looked away, and sniffed. "Sorry, but sometimes I miss him so much...." She sniffed again, but managed another smile. "Your grandpa invited me to stay for lunch, and I accepted. This is such a delightful setting, what with the green grass and all the trees and flowers. I can remember when Emma planted those rosebushes beside the arbor, and look at them now. Well, back to your grandpa. I told him I thought I could get Emma out of her writer's slump, but I don't want her to know that's why I'm here. Emma and I

go back a good long way, and I think I know her better than she knows herself."
She clapped her hands. "We need to make this whole thing festive and fun, and I know just how to do it."

Wes put the hot dogs on the grill, and sighed. "You're welcome to try whatever you want, Lolly. But I'd be mighty careful what I say, if I were you. One misplaced word, and she'll fly right off the handle. These days, you *look* at her wrong, and she'll fly off the handle."

A few minutes later, Emma walked out of the house, carrying glasses and a pitcher of lemonade on a tray. "Hello, Lolly," she said, putting the tray on the picnic table. "Would you like to join us for lunch?"

"I'd like that very much, Emma," Lolly said, kissing the air on either side of Emma's face in a "kiss-kiss" greeting. "You're probably wondering why I'm here. Well, I want to start writing my story, and just can't find the right place to begin. You're so far ahead of us, and you've gotten so professional, I thought you might have some suggestions. I was going to talk to you about it in class tonight, but then I found out you weren't coming, so here I am.''

Emma poured lemonade into four tall glasses, and said, "So what is your plot about?"

Lolly was about to answer Emma, when Gloria Anderson arrived, sweeping through the arbor, carrying a picnic basket over her arm. She gave Wes an engaging grin, and announced, "If I can't get you off on a picnic, the picnic will just have to come to you!" Her green eyes flickered over Emma, and settled on Lolly. "We haven't met. My name is Gloria Anderson."

Lolly's dark eyes were flickering over Gloria, too, who looked ravishing in a yellow sundress and sandals. She gritted her teeth. "My name is Lolly Peabody." She looped her arm through Wes's. "Wes and I are such good friends. Oh, and Emma, well, Emma and I went to school together. We're just like sisters. We tell each other *everything*. You must be new in town, hmmm?"

"I'm Rose Kelly's aunt," Gloria said,

also through clenched teeth. "I'd like to talk to you alone, Wes...."

"I have to tend to the hot dogs, Gloria."

"Oh, for goodness' sake, let *Emma* tend to the hot dogs. This is important!"

"And so was the little discussion we were having before you arrived," Lolly announced with a flip of her head.

Wes gave Emma a helpless shrug. "Will you watch the hot dogs, Emma? I'll only be a few minutes."

After they'd disappeared around the corner of the house, Lolly snapped, "Was I imagining things? Or did that woman have stars in her eyes when she looked at Wes?"

"You weren't imagining it," Emma muttered. "She's looking for a husband, and thinks Wes is the perfect candidate."

Lolly's eyes narrowed over Emma. "And how does Wes feel about that?"

"Flattered, but he hasn't let it go to his head. I'm the only one around here who lets things go to my head."

Jennifer spoke up. "Let's concentrate on your plot, Lolly, and forget about Gloria

Anderson. Grandfather can handle her. See? Here he comes, and he's alone."

Another shrug, but this time it was more sheepish than helpless. "Sorry about that," he said, "but that lady doesn't like to take no for an answer. Don't worry, Emma. I wasn't rude, but I got my point across."

"A little rudeness might be just what that woman needs!" Emma said with a snort.

"About your story, Lolly," Jennifer pressed, praying Gloria's sudden appearance wouldn't ruin the afternoon.

"Hold that thought," Wes said, "while I get the salad and condiments out of the kitchen."

Emma said she would help him, and after they'd gone into the house, Lolly whispered, "If I didn't know better, I'd say Emma is in love with your grandpa, and that it might even be mutual."

Jennifer grinned. "You're very perceptive, Lolly. And I'll admit their relationship has changed over the last couple of years, only they aren't aware of it. I don't know what's going to happen when they do, but I know it will be wonderful.''

Lolly sighed. "Because love is wonderful. Shhhh, here they come."

"Sorry for the interruption again," Wes said, "but the hot dogs are ready. Help yourself, Lolly."

Emma said, "About your story..."

Lolly spread mustard on a bun, and said, "Ah-ha. Well, it's the story about a lonely lady who is willing to do just about anything to get attention."

"Anything?" Emma asked incredulously.

"Well, not *anything*, but she really is creative. I haven't figured out exactly what she's going to do yet, but that's not my problem. I don't know where to begin. Should it be during her first caper? Or afterward?"

Emma frowned. "That depends on what you mean by 'caper.' That sounds like you're going to have her doing bad things, not creative things."

"Not really bad. Well, maybe borderline. She isn't a bad person. In fact, she has

The Pink Rabbit Caper

a heart of gold, but right now, it's a little tarnished because she's so lonely.''

"So why is she so lonely?" Wes asked.

"Because her husband passed away, and she was never blessed with children. She keeps busy, of course, and has a lot of friends, but it isn't the same."

Emma cleared her throat. "Judith told us that it's okay to write about what we know, but if we do, to make sure we put it into fiction. Is this going to be a story about you, Lolly?"

Lolly's long, long lashes swept her cheeks. "Well, maybe a little bit of it. I'll make her a lot stronger and braver than me, though, and put her in a lovely home, and surround her with lots of fancy furniture and pretty clothes. I think that'll be a good contrast, because even though she has everything, she's still lonely. Of course, she'll live quite a ways from town, so she'll have to have a vegetable garden. Oh, and lots and lots of red creeper roses.

"How did you know where to start your story, Emma? I know you must have come up with your plot first."

Emma dished up the fruit salad, and frowned. "You know, I can't remember how that went. I knew it was going to be a mystery, and I knew my protagonist was going to be a private detective.... I remember, now. I came up with the plot, first, and then worked out the beginning."

"And the clues?"

Emma shook her head. "I'm still trying to work them out, and a whole lot of loose ends. That's why I've got writer's block. I've suddenly run out of ideas, and the few I do manage to come up with seem silly."

Lolly took a bite of hot dog, and wiped her mouth with a paper napkin. "Well, I thought that clue where you had Jake wading in the creek was marvelous. Did you go to the creek yourself, to check it out?"

"No, it was all up here," Emma said, pointing to her head.

Lolly sighed. "I don't know if I'll be that fortunate. I'm afraid I might have to work out some of the capers myself, so I'll get the true feel for it."

"That sounds compelling," Wes said.

"And dangerous," Emma added.

The Pink Rabbit Caper

Lolly shook her head. "Oh, I won't do anything *dangerous,* just adventurous. Of course, my character might find a little danger along the way. Isn't it strange how everybody in the class is writing about something different? Our tastes are so varied. Nettie likes to write poetry—well, I can understand that, because I enjoy writing it, too. And then there is Tracy Madison, who is positively sesquipedalian."

"Sesqui-who?" Emma asked.

Lolly tittered. "It means she uses long, complicated words. My husband used to say that about me, because I'd try to learn a new word each day, and the more complicated, the better. For a long time, I thought sesquipedalian was some sort of Indian word. It wasn't until he was in the hospital, and the bills were piling up, and I was trying to negotiate with all the bill collectors, that I realized using short, to-the-point words was much more effective.

"And then we have you, Emma, who loves to read mysteries, and tries to figure out the clues. No wonder you decided to write a story full of clues. And boy, they aren't subtle, either. They are right there. You are a very clever lady, and I just know in no time at all, you're going to work through your writer's block." She frowned. "But that does bring one question to mind. John, Jr., is supposed to print your first installment in the paper on Sunday. Do you have enough to give him?"

"More than enough," Emma replied. "I've already given him the first five installments, so all I can do is pray that by the time I have to give him the last five, I'll be back at the typewriter."

Lolly leaned back in the lawn chair, and crossed her long legs. "You know, maybe we should think about getting a computer. Tracy Madison has one, and to hear her talk, it's the best thing to happen to a writer since the electric pencil sharpener. I don't know what you're using, but my old typewriter is on its last legs." She looked at her watch. "Oh, dear! I had no idea it was getting so late. I still have to go to the market, and stop by the library. I want to check out a book on Calico's history. All ambience for my story, of course.

The Pink Rabbit Caper

"This has really been delightful, and I appreciate your hospitality."

Lolly was still in the process of leaving five minutes later, but Jennifer had excused herself and had gone into the house. She was afraid Lolly might notice the expression on her face, which could only be called unadulterated shock.

Now Jennifer was standing in the kitchen, waiting for Wes and Emma, and trying to remember when the thought had hit her—when she'd realized almost all their questions had been answered, and in a most unique way. She guessed it was when Lolly had mentioned the red creeper roses. But, oh, there had been so many other hints dropped along the way, and Jennifer felt the excitement build. She didn't know how, or why, but without a doubt, Lolly Peabody had written the notes.

Chapter Seven

By the time Wes and Emma walked into the kitchen, Jennifer had all the hints, which translated into clues, written down on a sheet of paper. The words swooshed out of her mouth in a tumble. "Lolly has been sending us the notes, and I can prove it. It all fits. Look!"

Wes and Emma read over the list, and shook their heads.

"Oh no," Emma finally whispered. "I don't want to believe it, and yet there it is, just as plain as day."

Jennifer rushed on. "I think I finally realized the truth when Lolly mentioned the red creeper roses, which are the same kind of roses we found on Latona B. Marshell's grave. Then there is the letter I received today, and where it says, 'I swear to you on my great-grandmother's grave.' I think Latona Marshell is Lolly's great-grandmother. Oh, and I just looked up Lolly's address, and guess what? It's 4444 Beechnut Road. Norman Fuller's address is 4446 and Nettie's is 4448. Four fours, might translate into four doughnuts, though I don't know why they had to be chocolate-covered.''

"I do," Emma said. "Lolly remembered the argument we had years ago. We were getting things ready for a school Halloween party, and we were on the refreshment committee. Lolly wanted to order glazed doughnuts, and I wanted chocolate-covered. The teacher ended up coming to our rescue, and made us realize we could order some of each, along with cake, jelly, and powdered sugar, and then everybody would be happy. The fact that it's Lolly, also explains why that description in the letter seemed so familiar to me. A long stretch of road, a tree on a hill, and a row of corn. She was describing her house. I haven't been out there in years, but I remember the long, narrow road, and the giant elm tree on a hill not far from Lolly's house."

"What about the corn?" Wes asked.

"Homer always planted one row of corn along the property line to the west, for a windbreak during the dry and windy late summer months. I remember Lolly telling me how foolish it was, and how much she wished he'd plant a row of trees instead."

"Now all we have to do is tie in the water filtration plant. . . ."

"I can do that," Wes said.

Emma nodded. "And so can I. Homer worked at the plant before he retired."

"Then it's just like she said in the letter," Jennifer said. "It was all right there. All we had to do was put it together."

Emma sat down, and sighed. "Now all we have to do is figure out why."

Jennifer said, "Why Lolly wrote the notes? I think it's obvious, Emma. She's lonely, and she's looking for attention, just like the protagonist in her story. That sounds like a cry for help to me, and when you take into consideration she's been carrying around that pink rabbit Homer gave her . . . Oh, it's so sad!''

"Or it's ingenious," Wes offered. "In the first note, she also said there was a body buried somewhere in Calico, and made it quite clear that it wasn't in the cemetery."

Jennifer stared at her grandfather. "Are you suggesting Lolly killed her husband?"

Wes shrugged. "If all the clues she gave us are legitimate, why would she toss in one that wasn't?"

"Is it possible this is her way of acting out a delayed confession?" Emma asked.

"It's possible," Wes said, "but it also leaves one very big unanswered question. *Why* she killed him. They always seemed to get along pretty good, though I'll admit Homer was a little strange."

Emma snorted. "And Lolly isn't? They made a good pair, those two, but you're wrong, Wes. They used to fight all the time."

A smile tugged at the corners of Wes's mouth. "We fight all the time, too, Emma, but that doesn't mean you're going to kill me, and plant me in the rose garden."

Emma ignored Wes's attempt at humor, and asked, "Do you remember what happened when Homer died?"

Wes nodded. "He *supposedly* took sick while they were visiting friends in Omaha, and he *supposedly* died in an Omaha hospital."

"That's right, but the body wasn't shipped to Calico. *Supposedly*, he was buried in Omaha. But what if he didn't die in Omaha? What if Homer was killed right here? That's it! That's the answer to my writing dilemma, too. I'll have everybody think all five husbands were out of town at the time of their deaths, but of course they weren't...." She shook her head. "You know, I don't care all that much about finishing the story now, in light of this real-life tragedy."

Jennifer said, "We're only speculating, Emma. Maybe Lolly only put that part about a buried body in that first note because of the plot in your story."

"Emma's story could have also given Lolly the idea to turn her confession into a mystery game, too," Wes reasoned. "I know it's still only conjecture at this point, but I think I'd better call the sheriff. I have no idea how he'll want to handle it, but he has to be brought up to date. I'll use the phone in my study."

While Wes was in the study making the call, Jennifer and Emma went out to sit on the front porch, where they could enjoy the afternoon sun, smell the sweet scent of flowers, and pray they were wrong. But even the warmth of the sun couldn't keep the chill out of their hearts.

Fifteen minutes later, Wes walked out on the porch with heavy steps. "I hated making that call," he said wearily, "but if there is even a remote chance . . ." He shook his head. "The sheriff is more inclined to believe Lolly is only playing a game, but he's going to put in some calls to Omaha just the same."

"To find out if Homer was actually buried in Omaha?"

"That's right, sweetheart. It was a few years ago, so it might take some time. Meanwhile, I think we should go out to Lolly's house, and do some poking around."

"I don't understand."

"Well, for one thing, the sheriff wants a sample from her typewriter."

"I can go to class tonight, and try to get a sample," Jennifer said.

"Short of swiping it, I don't see how, so I think we'd better go out to the house, and come up with something creative...."

Emma said, "I have an idea. Tell her that Ken Hering is writing a story for the newspaper about the women in Calico's history, and ask her about her great-grandmother. If she says Latona B. Marshell was her great-grandmother, you can ask her to type up a little bio."

Wes looked at Emma, and raised a brow. "For that shrewd little scheme, you'd better say a dozen prayers before you go to bed tonight, Emma."

Emma flushed rosy pink, and shrugged. "So, can you come up with something better?"

"Unfortunately, I can't." Wes looked at his watch. "It's only two o'clock. I realize Lolly is going to the writing class tonight, but if we leave now, we'll have plenty of time." He looked at Jennifer. "I'll go warm up the car, sweetheart, unless you'd rather take the Jeep."

"Your car is fine, Grandfather. . . ."

Emma frowned. "And you don't think Lolly is going to think it's fishy when the two of you pop up on her doorstep, after just saying good-bye to her not more than a half hour ago?"

Wes grinned. "She said she was going to the market, and then the library. That should give us plenty of time to poke around before she gets home." The grin widened. "Uh-huh. You remember the sunglasses somebody left in church last Sunday? We'll take them along and pretend we thought they were hers. I know, Emma. You don't have to look at me like that. It's a dozen extra prayers for me tonight, too."

After Wes had gone to warm up the car, Emma let out an audible sigh. "That isn't what I was thinking at all. I was thinking about what a wonderful Jake Lamont he would make, and how he'd look in a pinstriped suit."

"Jake Lamont's trademark attire?" Jennifer asked with a smile.

Emma flushed again. "Dark gray, with lighter gray pinstripes, white shirt, and a dark maroon tie. With Wes's white hair, I think he would look absolutely gorgeous."

"And you're gorgeous," Jennifer said, giving Emma a hug. "Wish us luck?"

Emma nodded, but Jennifer could see the concern in her eyes. Luck didn't enter into it. Just the heartfelt knowledge that her longtime friend might be a murderer.

Jennifer hadn't been out on Beechnut Road in a long time, either, but now, seeing the long road and the giant elm tree standing like a sentinel to the left of Lolly's white farmhouse, she felt chills skipping up and down her back.

Wes parked in the gravel driveway, and

took a deep breath. "So far so good. If we work fast, we might get the whole yard covered before she comes home."

Jennifer looked out at the wide expanse of lawn surrounded by numerous trees and flower beds, and asked, "What are we supposed to be looking for, Grandfather?"

Wes stuffed the sunglasses in his shirt pocket. "Anything that might look like a burial plot, I would imagine. Not that I think she put up a headstone, you understand, but I would think she put up some kind of a marker."

"And the ten acres of farmland behind the house?"

"I don't think she would've buried Homer in an area that gets plowed under every year." He gritted his teeth. "You take the back, and I'll poke around out here."

Jennifer made her way around the house, and followed the sloping lawn down to the little bridge that spanned the creek. On the other side, there was a gentle rise that was covered with iris and peonies. It was a well-cared-for garden, and nothing seemed out of place. From where she was standing, she could see Norman Fuller's house through the trees, and the pastureland beyond.

After checking out every possible spot, Jennifer finally sat down on a redwood bench in a small picnic area near the creek, and sighed. If Lolly had killed her husband, Jennifer was convinced he wasn't buried here.

Movement near the house caught Jennifer's eye. It was her grandfather and Lolly, and they were talking and smiling as they made their way toward her.

When they reached her, Jennifer tried for a smile. "I just couldn't resist sitting here for a while, Lolly. It's such a beautiful spot."

Lolly sat down in a redwood chair, and sighed. "Yes, it is. It was one of Homer's favorite spots. . . ." She cleared her throat. "I want to thank you both for coming all this way, just to return a pair of sunglasses you thought were mine. Unfortunately, they aren't."

"Guess we'll just have to put them in

the lost and found at the church,'' Wes said casually.

Lolly dimpled up at Wes. "And I want to thank you for carrying in my groceries, Wes. Are you sure you won't stay and have a cup of tea?"

"Maybe some other time, Lolly." He winked at Jennifer. "Are you ready, sweetheart? We told Emma we wouldn't be gone long."

"I'll walk to the car with you," Lolly was saying, but Jennifer was more intent on the curious expression on her grandfather's face. Nor had he said anything about the story Ken Hering was supposedly writing for the newspaper, which would have enabled them to get a sample from Lolly's typewriter.

They were walking along the pathway beside the house, on their way to the car, when Lolly stopped and said, "If you'll look through the trees to your right, you'll be able to see Normal Fuller's wonderful rose garden. He has a special knack for growing cabbage roses and creepers, and I'm just green with envy, because I simply can't grow a decent rose, and believe me, I've tried them all. Homer always thought it was because we have so much shade." She sighed heavily. "I don't think there is anything more wonderful than a sweet scent of roses on a warm spring night."

Jennifer could see part of Norman Fuller's rose garden, and tried very hard to act nonchalant, but it was hardly the way she felt. Lolly had mentioned "creepers." Red creeper roses? And was that where she'd gotten the bouquet to put on the grave?

Wes took it one step further, though he waited until they were in the car before he said, "You don't suppose Lolly killed Homer and planted him in *Norman*'s rose garden, do you?"

Jennifer leaned her head against the seat, and closed her eyes. "Or maybe Norman Fuller killed his wife, and buried her in the rose garden."

"And Lolly saw him do it? Boy, oh boy, sweetheart, I don't know if I can buy that, either. I'm having enough trouble with Lolly and Homer."

"But nobody has seen Norman's wife in

ages, and you have to admit that's pretty strange. You remember what he told you the first time he came to church without her?"

"Uh-huh. He said she was visiting friends in Tennessee."

"And last fall, he told me she was visiting friends in Kansas. And what about all those times Emma has asked him about his wife? He says she's either off visiting somebody, or she isn't feeling well. And don't forget Nettie, who has maintained all along he has his wife stashed away, living on bread and water."

"I think Nettie meant that in jest, sweetheart."

"Maybe, but what if? Maybe the sheriff should pay Norman Fuller a visit."

"And say what? That he knows Norman killed his wife, and now he wants to know where he buried her? There is no way the sheriff could do that, without some sort of proof."

"But the sheriff could talk to him, couldn't he? At least feel him out?"

"I suppose. I'll talk to the sheriff, and

see what he says. I have to give him this, anyway." He handed Jennifer a crumpled sheet of paper, and grinned. "I guess that proves I'm not just another pretty face."

Jennifer stared at the typewritten words with the bold, slightly crooked E, and exclaimed, "How on earth did you get this!"

"When I helped Lolly in with the groceries, I saw the typewriter on the kitchen table, and the wastepaper basket full of wadded-up papers. So, while she had her head in the refrigerator, I plucked one of them out of the trash and stuffed it in my pocket."

"That's amazing!"

The grin widened. "So, do we have a matching E? I didn't get a chance to look at it. . . . Jennifer?"

Jennifer blinked. "Sorry, but I was reading."

"Does it have the infamous E?"

"It does, and a whole lot more. This isn't part of Lolly's story. It's the beginning of another clue."

Wes took a deep breath. "And?"

Red creeper roses cover the ground. Look close, and what you thought was lost will be found. Ashes to ashes, dust to dust . . .

"And that's where it ends."

Wes sucked in his cheeks. "So, between the clues Lolly gave us when she was talking about Norman Fuller's rose garden, and that note, she all but pinpointed the location."

Jennifer couldn't help but shudder. "Looks like. What's going to happen now?"

"I'm afraid it's out of our hands, sweetheart. Shall we go talk to the sheriff?"

Jennifer shuddered again, and nodded.

Chapter Eight

"If there is a body buried in Norman Fuller's rose garden, it isn't his wife," the sheriff said, squinting against the late-afternoon sun.

They'd caught the sheriff just as he was leaving his office for the day, and now they were standing beside his patrol car, waiting for him to explain.

Finally, the sheriff shifted uncomfortably from foot to foot, and shrugged. "Under the circumstances, I guess I haven't got much choice but to tell you the truth, even though Norman swore me to secrecy. The truth is, his wife is in a sanitarium in Lincoln, and has been for over three years. She has Alzheimer's, and Norman just didn't want anybody to know about it."

"I'm mighty sorry to hear that," Wes said, "though I don't understand his reasoning. Alzheimer's isn't something to be ashamed of. It's like any other debilitating disease, and someday they might even find a cure."

Jennifer spoke up. "But there has always been a stigma attached to it, Grandfather, and there are still a lot of people who believe if you have Alzheimer's, you are mentally insane. That poor man. What a terrible thing to have to go through alone."

Wes sighed. "Well, then, I guess that pretty much tells us who is buried in the rose garden."

The sheriff studied the last partial clue Wes had picked up out of Lolly's wastebasket, and shook his head. "I still think she's playing some sort of a game, though I don't suppose it would hurt to take a look at Norman's rose garden. The note says to 'look close,' so maybe she's left a visible clue." He looked at his watch. "Still have a few hours left before dark, if you want to do it now."

"The sooner the better," Wes said. "Otherwise, nobody will be able to sleep tonight."

"Uh-huh. Well, I'll call Ida, and tell her I'll be late, and then I'd better call Norman, so he'll be prepared."

Wes nodded. "We'll follow you in my car, Jim. Hmmmm, I'd better call Emma, too...." His eyes settled on Jennifer. "You okay, sweetheart? You look a little peaked."

"I'm fine," Jennifer said, managing a smile. But of course she wasn't, because just the thought of finding Homer's body in Norman Fuller's rose garden was more than unsettling.

Norman's house was smaller than Lolly's, but was similar in design, though it didn't have the sweeping front porch. Nor were there any signs of tender loving care. The house and the surrounding garden looked unkempt, as did the gaunt-looking man who was waiting for them when they pulled up the long, narrow driveway.

Norman, who did indeed look like Norman Bates, hitched his trousers, and frowned. "I always said that lady was crazy. Been living here going on seven years now, and not even that grove of peachleaf willows between us can block out what I hear going on. Loud music, her caterwauling that's supposed to be singing, talking to herself all the time, and the parties far into the night."

The sheriff frowned. "Parties?"

"Yeah. She gives parties, only nobody comes. It's just Lolly, all dressed up in those old-fashioned fancy clothes, dancing out on the lawn until midnight. Went over there one night, to tell her to knock it off and go to bed, so what does she do? She turns up the music, and hands me a glass of champagne. The only time I get any peace is when the weather turns cold, and she has to stay inside."

Jennifer swallowed around the lump in her throat. "She sounds lonely, Mr. Fuller."

"Yeah, well, I'm lonely, too," Norman said, leading the way around the house. "But that don't mean I have to act like a crazy person."

"Did you take a look at the rose garden after I called you?" the sheriff asked.

"No way. If she's planted Homer in my garden, you're gonna be the one who digs him up, not me." They'd reached the rose garden, and he waved a hand. "Sorry about all the weeds. My wife was the one who took care of the roses. Now it don't seem to matter whether they get weeded or not. Nothing seems to matter...." His words trailed off, and his breath came out in a low whistle. "Well, will you look at that!"

"Boy, oh boy," Wes said, taking Jennifer's hand. "Is that obvious, or what?"

Jennifer stared at the small area of freshly turned earth between the cabbage roses and the red creepers, and uttered, "The cultivated area is too small. A body couldn't possibly be buried there. More important, the area shouldn't be cultivated at all. Homer died a long time ago, so by now, that part of the ground wouldn't look any different than the rest of it.''

"Unless she dug up just enough to let us know where he's buried," Wes said.

The sheriff rolled up his sleeves. "Do you have a shovel I can use, Norman?"

While Norman went to get the shovel, Jennifer saw the movement through the trees, and whispered, "Lolly is watching us, Grandfather. No, don't turn around. She's standing on the pathway in just about the same spot where she pointed out Norman's rose garden. It's almost like she knew this was going to happen. . . ."

"I spotted her five minutes ago," the sheriff muttered. "And to tell you the truth, I don't like the idea of her being over there alone. If Homer is buried here, she might think this is what she wants to happen, but if she changes her mind at the last minute . . ."

Jennifer said, "You think she might run? Well, you don't have to worry about that, Sheriff Cody. She's on her way over, and wait until you see the smile on her face."

Lolly reached the rose garden at the

same time Norman returned with the shovel, and the scowl on his face was as dark as Lolly's smile was bright. She clapped her hands, and her eyes twinkled with merriment. "I don't know if my clues were *that* good, or you folks are just *that* smart, but to tell you the truth, I didn't expect *this* to happen until you got the last clue. I was going to send it to you tomorrow."

Jennifer reached in her purse, and pulled out the crumpled slip of paper. "You mean this clue, Lolly? "Red creeper roses cover the ground. Look close, and what you thought was lost will be found. Ashes to ashes, dust to dust . . . ' That's where it ends."

Lolly's response was instant. "Oh, my, how on earth did you get that?"

"I plucked it out of your wastebasket when I helped you in with the groceries," Wes said.

Her mouth dimpled at the corners. "Well, aren't you the sly one, Wesley Gray."

Jennifer asked, "What else were you going to put in the clue, Lolly?"

"'Ashes to ashes, dust to dust, your final resting place will be close to me, and amid the red creeper roses you loved so much.' But I wasn't happy with that, and thought I could do better. That's why I tossed it in the trash."

The sheriff leaned on the shovel handle, and scowled. "So if I start digging, am I going to find your husband's body?"

"In a roundabout way. You're going to find an urn full of Homer's ashes, and my pink bunny. Homer gave me that bunny the Easter before he died, and I hated to part with it, but I didn't want him to go to his final resting place lonely, either."

Finally beginning to understand what was happening here, Jennifer managed to get out, "Your husband was cremated in Omaha, and you've had his ashes all this time?"

Lolly sighed. "Yes, I have, and for the longest time, I simply didn't know what to do with them. I thought about having them scattered, like so many people do these days, and I thought about having the urn interred at the cemetery. And then the miracle happened. I signed up for that writing class, Emma came up with that wonderful plot, and I knew exactly what I had to do. Homer loved a good mystery, so what would be better than having him go to his final resting place, smack dab in the middle of one? One that I'd created? I buried the urn the day after Emma read the beginning of her story in class. Norman wasn't home, so I had my own little service right here. I cried some, when I patted down the last scoop of dirt, but oh, the fragrance of the roses was wonderful, and it was such a soft, sweet day. The ground was warm, too, and I just knew he was being embraced by God's hand.''

Tears rolled down her cheeks, and she looked away.

When the sheriff spoke, his voice was hoarse. ''Well, I'm sorry to say, you can't go around burying people, or their ashes, wherever you want, Lolly. We've got rules and regulations.''

Lolly sniffed. ''I guess I knew that all

along, but this was something I just had to do, Sheriff. This was the only place I knew of that had red creeper roses, besides Calico Park, and I couldn't very well bury him there."

Wes spoke up. "You've caused a lot of frayed nerves and sleepless hours, Lolly."

Lolly's pretty mouth turned down. "I'm truly sorry about that. That was never my intention. I thought you'd all get a kick out of following my clues, just like the town is getting a kick out of Emma's little story. Everybody loves a good mystery, and..."

"Not everybody," Norman Fuller muttered, "but I guess I understand." His sigh was ragged. "If nothing else, I understand your loneliness."

Lolly snorted. "Well, with Agnes gone so much of the time, I can understand that. Why don't you tell her to stay home where she belongs? Doesn't she realize how important it is for you to try to share every minute of every day together? To tell you the truth, I can't remember the last time I saw her. Where is she now, Norman? Visiting friends in Texas?"

Norman's eyes filled with tears. "Agnes has Alzheimer's, and has been in a sanitarium in Lincoln for the last three years, Lolly."

Lolly sucked in her breath. "Oh, Norman! I'm so sorry. Why didn't you say something?"

Norman shrugged. "Why bother you or anybody else with my problems?"

"But don't you see? That's what friends are for. I'll admit there have been times I've been so lonely I could hardly stand it, but I do have some friends, and I don't know what I'd do without them."

The sheriff said, "Ahem. It's getting late, so I suggest we'd better decide what to do about Homer."

Lolly knelt down, and gave the ground a loving pat. "I guess I'll have him interred at the cemetery. I'll call J. C. Fowler first thing in the morning, and make the necessary arrangements."

Norman blew his nose, and looked at the sheriff. "Would it be okay if Homer stays here until it's time to move him?"

The sheriff returned, "I don't have any

problems with that, as long as it doesn't take too long.''

Lolly's smile was beautiful, and she gave the sheriff a quick hug. ''Thank you, Sheriff. And thank you, Norman. Now, if I can get Wes, Emma, and Jennifer to forgive me . . .''

Wes gave Lolly a compassionate smile. ''There's nothing to forgive, Lolly. To be honest with you, I've rather enjoyed all the supersleuthing we've been doing. I'm just glad it turned out the way it did.''

The sheriff said, ''Well, I'm not surprised it turned out the way it did. I thought all along it was some sort of a game, thought out by one whopping creative mind.'' He shook his head. ''You and Emma Morrison. You two would make quite a team.

''Now, I'm out of here. Call me when you get your plans finalized, Lolly, and I'll do whatever I can to help.''

After the sheriff had gone, Lolly smiled brightly, and said, ''I've fixed a wonderful Irish stew, if you'd all like to join me.''

''Sorry,'' Wes said, ''but Emma is expecting us home for dinner. But we'd sure like a rain check.''

Norman stuffed his hands in his pockets, and a flush touched his cheeks. "I haven't had Irish stew in ages, Lolly, so I wouldn't mind joining you for dinner at all. Is there anything I can bring?"

Wes winked at Jennifer, and the warmth of his smile touched her heart. Two lonely people wouldn't be lonely tonight, and it was wonderful.

It was a warn, sunny Saturday, and the perfect day for a potluck supper, which was also going to be a celebration of Homer Peabody's life. It had been a week since that day the final clue led them to Norman Fuller's rose garden, and now, after a lovely memorial service at the cemetery, the social hall at the church was full of friends and well-wishers, who all wanted to be a part of this special day.

It had been Norman Fuller's suggestion that red creeper roses be planted on Homer's plot at the cemetery, and it had been

Emma's idea to fill the social hall with the sweet-smelling flowers.

Very pleased, and looking quite lovely in a soft blue dress with a drop waist, and with a blue feathered headband around her silver hair, Lolly was relaxing at a corner table with Emma. A few of the latecomers helped themselves to the succulent assortment of dishes, which included lasagna, baked beans, salads, fried chicken, casseroles, and cakes.

Jennifer and Ken Hering were sitting near an open window, enjoying the soft breeze, the afterglow of the enjoyable meal, and the camaraderie, when Ken looked around and sighed. "It's funny how things turn out, and how one chain of events can bring people together. And you know, I think this is the first time I've seen Norman Fuller with a smile on his face."

"That's because he's found a special friend in Lolly, and he's realized that loneliness is only a state of mind. He had so many friends who would have helped him, had he only reached out."

"And tomorrow, the town will have

something else to talk about when they read the second installment of Emma's story in the newspaper. I read it in advance, and it's terrific. Gripping. More importantly, she's over her slump, and plans on finishing it.''

Jennifer grinned at him. ''Well, while we're on the subject, Emma has an important announcement to make later on.''

''What kind of an announcement?''

''You'll see.''

''Is it good news?''

''It's wonderful news.''

''Uh-huh, well, I have the feeling this is going to be a day full of surprises.''

''And what do you mean by that?''

''You'll see.''

''Ken!''

He gave her a hug. ''Just be patient, pretty vet lady.''

''Do you know what Ken has up his sleeve?'' Jennifer asked Wes a few minutes later.

They were standing near the dessert table, and Wes's blue eyes twinkled. "Maybe a slice of apple pie?"

"I'm serious, Grandfather! He said this was going to be a day full of surprises, but wouldn't even give me a clue."

"I know you're serious, sweetheart, but you're just going to have to wait."

"So, you *do* know!"

He raised his hand. "Let's sit down. Emma is about to make her announcement."

All eyes were on Emma as she made her way to the front of the room, so there was no need to get anybody's attention. She began by thanking everybody for attending the memorial service and the potluck, and then took a deep breath. "First of all, I want you all to know, I finished my story last night...." Cheers went up, and Emma's face dimpled with pleasure. "I know, that's about the way I feel. As most of you know, I've had quite a time with it, and I've finally figured out why. Anybody can learn to write, but not everybody can be a writer, and there is a big difference. I'm not a writer, and never will be. I simply had a story to tell, and now it's finished, and I can get on with the things that are really important...."

There were a few groans and moans, but Emma pressed on. "... And another project that is even more exciting. I can honestly say that Lolly's great-grandmother, Latona B. Marshall, was the inspiration for this, but it wasn't until I remembered a conversation I had with Jennifer and Wes, that I realized what I had to do. I won't go into the details of that conversation, because it was full of conniving plots and schemes, because at the time we were busy running all over town, following Lolly's masterful clues. But one thing came out of that conversation. A book should be written about the women in Calico's history, and Lolly and I are going to write it."

Cheers and applause again, and it was deafening.

Lolly made her way up to Emma's side, and raised her hand. "But we're not going to let it take over our lives. We'll approach it realistically and professionally, and block out a little bit of time every day to work on it. We won't have a deadline, so it really doesn't matter how long it takes to write, and for the most part, our biggest chore will be in compiling the necessary information."

Emma spoke up. "And to do that, we're going to need your help. Lolly's great-grandmother was a wonderful part of Calico's history, and there must be many more of you who have grandmothers and great-grandmothers who will be able to add their own wonderful nuances to a book that can only be held dear to all our hearts."

"If you have anything to contribute, feel free to call us," Lolly said.

"What about a publisher?" somebody asked.

Emma smiled. "We don't expect it to be a best-seller. And more than likely only the people who live in Calico will be interested in reading it, so if we have to, we'll publish it ourselves, and make sure everybody in Calico gets a copy."

"What about a title?" Ken asked.

Emma said, "We're open for suggestions on that, too."

Wes spoke up. "Maybe we can have some sort of a contest. Same with the cover art."

A few minutes later, as the two ladies were mobbed by the crowd and dozens of ideas, Jennifer pulled Ken off to the side, and whispered, "So, Mr. Smarty Pants, can you top that?"

Ken looked at his watch, and grinned. "I think you're going to find out in about two minutes." He glanced over her shoulder, toward the front door. "No, make that right about now."

Jennifer turned around and gasped. "Oh, yikes! Is that who I think it is?"

Ken beamed. "None other than Paul Stanford. Mystery writer extraordinaire. Author of such notable books as *The Headless Rider of Bayberry Street, Countdown with Death, Shadows at Midnight,* and *The House Without Windows.*"

Jennifer shook her head. "He's Emma's favorite author."

"I know." Ken waved a hand at the tall, distinguished-looking man, but Emma had already spied him, and let out a squeal.

The Pink Rabbit Caper

Pandemonium followed, and it was a good ten minutes later before Emma had settled down enough to introduce Paul Stanford to the crowd, and explain why he was there. And even then, Ken had to step in, and help her along the way.

"It was really simple," Ken said. "I knew Paul Stanford was going to be in Omaha for a book signing, and sent a copy of Emma's story—first five installments—to the bookstore ahead of time, with a letter of introduction, and an invitation to come to Calico this weekend, as my guest. To tell you the truth, I didn't think I'd hear from him, so I was more than surprised when he called and accepted my invitation."

Paul Stanford spoke up. "And it was my pleasure. I found Emma's story more than intriguing, and can't wait to read the rest of it. But in all honesty, that isn't the only reason I'm here. Ken also sent me a clipping from *The Calico Review* about Lolly Peabody, her late husband, and the pink rabbit, and I'd like to turn her compelling story into a book."

Another squeal, and this time, it was from Lolly.

Paul smiled. "I'll be here for a few days, so I'm sure that will give us enough time to reach some sort of an agreement, Lolly, and in the meantime, I can read the rest of Emma's story, and enjoy all that Calico has to offer. Supposedly, my great-grandmother lived here in 1873, and it's always been my intention to come here for a visit."

Jennifer was standing with Wes, and put her head on his shoulder. "Would you say it's a small world, or what?"

Wes chuckled. "I'd say it's a small world. I would also say that Paul Stanford doesn't know what he's in for. Did you see the look on Emma's face when he mentioned his great-grandmother?"

"I did, and it was wonderful. She claims this project isn't going to get out of hand, but I'm not so sure."

"Uh-huh, and that's why we're going to hire outside help for the summer."

"Oh, no, not again!"

Wes gave her a hug. "This time it will

be different, sweetheart. The Mullers' granddaughter just graduated from high school, and because of some family problems, she'll be staying with the Mullers until further notice. She also wants a part-time job, and I don't think it would hurt to try her out. She's energetic and sweet and seems like a super kid, so what have we got to lose?"

"Transportation? It's a long way out to the Muller farm."

"She has her own car. She's coming to church tomorrow, so we can talk to her then."

"Does Emma know about it?"

"She does, and she's agreeable. Just as long as she isn't another middle-aged female, looking for a husband."

Jennifer giggled. "Speaking of Gloria, have you seen her lately?"

"Nope, and I'm not likely to, now. I heard she got into a hassle with Rose, and left town." He gave an audible sigh. "Look at Emma. Have you ever seen her more radiant? We have to give her all the love and support we can, sweetheart. And we have to make the best of things, and accept what can't be changed. And this time around, I know we'll get it right.''

Jennifer knew they would get it right, too, because they were a family, surrounded by love.